Ruined by a Rake

An All's Fair in Love Novella

By Erin Knightley

Dedication

To Catherine Gayle, for putting up with me and my endless questions. And for Kirk, even though you're entirely too nice to ever be a decent rake.

ISBN: 1493522175
ISBN-13: 978-1493522170

Books By Erin Knightley:

The SEALED WITH A KISS Series
More Than a Stranger
A Taste for Scandal
Flirting with Fortune
Miss Mistletoe – A Penguin eSpecial

The PRELUDE TO A KISS Series
The Baron Next Door (June 2014)

The ALL'S FAIR IN LOVE Series (Novellas)
Ruined by a Rake
Scandalized by a Scoundrel

Contents

Prologue

$\mathcal{N}$icolas, say hello to your new cousin."

Eleanor Abbington glanced up sharply at her new aunt's statement. How had she been singled out? With the entire family gathered in the courtyard of Malcolm Manor to meet Uncle Robert's new wife and her son, it didn't seem fair that Eleanor should find herself the center of attention.

Aunt Lavinia smiled as she glanced back and forth between them, her golden eyebrows raised in two perfect arches of expectation. "Eleanor is closest to you in age, only two years your senior."

Only two years? That was more than a quarter of the boy's lifetime. For some reason it annoyed her that a seven-year-old was nearly as tall as she. He looked rather like a giraffe, actually, with his long and spindly limbs. Sighing, Eleanor waited for him to say something, to get these forced niceties out of the way. But he didn't. Instead, he just stood there, staring down at his shiny brown shoes and letting the silence stretch.

Tittering like a squeaky field mouse, Aunt Lavinia turned to Eleanor. "I think he's shy with all these new people. Be a good girl and give your new cousin a kiss."

A *kiss*? Eleanor tried not to make a face, but it wasn't easy. She couldn't possibly expect her to kiss this strange boy. Just because Aunt Lavinia had *called* him her cousin, didn't make it so. She had overheard Mama talking to Aunt Margaret; she knew that Aunt Lavinia was just a silver-tongue widow—though her tongue looked quite pink to Eleanor—who had somehow managed to fool Uncle Robert, the revered Earl of Malcolm, into marrying her.

Eleanor sent a pleading look to her mother. Mama cut a glance to her new sister-in-law, her mouth pinched and her brow lowered in the same sort of disapproving expression she gave the dog when it slipped inside with muddy paws, but she didn't intervene on Eleanor's behalf.

At her side, Libby watched with rounded eyes, leaning into their mother's skirts. For once, Eleanor was envious of her little sister. No one expected a toddler to

2

have to do such a thing. Or even a five-year-old, for that matter, though William, her *real* cousin, didn't seem as though he'd mind such a fate, peering up in adoration at his new stepbrother as he was.

"Eleanor," her mother said in warning.

Fine.

Sighing hugely, Eleanor stepped forward, reluctance weighing her feet like stones. Still Nicolas didn't look up. He simply stood there, letting his shaggy hair hang down across his forehead. Great—not only did she get a cousin she didn't want, but he was rude to boot. Didn't he know you should face someone when being forced to meet?

Pursing her mouth into a kiss that put her lips as far from her body as she could manage, she leaned forward, aiming for his freckled cheek. He smelled like wind and sunshine, which was better than the dirt and sweat smell she expected of a boy. Just when she was about to graze his cheek, he turned, quick as a whip, and smacked his lips to hers.

She sputtered and jumped back, wiping her whole arm across her violated lips. "Ew! Mama, he *kissed* me!"

For the first time since he arrived, Nicolas looked her right in the eye. He was grinning like the fool he

3

ERIN KNIGHTLEY

was, his pale green gaze dancing with smug merriment. "*I* was just standing here. *You* were the one who kissed *me*."

"Not on the *lips*," Eleanor said, spitting the words out along with the taste of him. "That's disgusting."

"Eleanor!" Mama barked, grabbing her by the arm and tugging her back sharply. "Mind your manners, young lady."

Mind *her* manners? She was the one who had been accosted by the little ruffian! But with Mama's fingers already digging into her upper arm, Eleanor knew better than to say what she was thinking. "Yes, ma'am," she mumbled, all the while leveling furious, narrowed eyes on Nicolas.

Did he appear even the tiniest bit contrite? Not even a little. As the adults went on with their greetings, she wrinkled her nose, telling him as clearly as she could manage that she did *not* like him, cousin or not.

His grin only widened, and then he winked at her. Winked!

Eleanor's mouth dropped open, which only made him look that much more pleased with himself. Of all the… she snapped her head to the side, refusing to give him the attention he so clearly craved. Even with her

4

gaze averted, she just *knew* he was still watching her, his infuriatingly smug grin still in place. So he thought he had bested her, did he?

Well, they'd see about that.

Chapter One

Fifteen years later

Oh Lord, she was trapped.

Standing in the center of the sun-dappled folly overlooking the rolling hills of her uncle's estate, Eleanor suddenly realized exactly what was about to happen. *Don't say it. Please don't say it.*

"Miss Abbington, will you consent to be my wife?" Across from her, Lord Kensington stood perfectly erect, his thick eyebrows raised in polite query.

Drat, drat, *drat.* Eleanor bit her lip, dismay settling like a brick in her stomach. Or was it dread? Why hadn't the man listened to her when she had told him in every way possible that she was happy in her situation, and had no plans to change it?

Better yet, why had she been so utterly oblivious to his intentions when she agreed to the walk in the first place? Now she was stuck, with no other choice than to be blunt. "Oh, my. I am sorry, my lord, but I am afraid I must decline your kind offer."

Silence reigned for the space of ten seconds, broken only by the nearby oak leaves rattling in the light wind as Lord Kensington absorbed her response. In those moments, the spacious, open-air folly seemed to shrink to the size of a cupboard, making it difficult for Eleanor to put enough space between her and her completely unwanted suitor.

"I beg your pardon?"

She tilted her head the slightest bit and tried to infuse compassion into her posture and expression. "My apologies, Lord Kensington, but my answer is no. I will not marry you."

What a fool she'd been to let it come to this. Yes, she'd known her uncle strongly favored a match between them, but this was only the second day Kensington had been at Malcolm Manor, for heaven's sake. The rest of the guests would arrive tomorrow, at which time the house party would officially begin. Did he feel that he had to rush things in order to get a leg up on the

7

competition?

Ugh, as if a houseful of boring members of Parliament would tempt her.

"But…" He trailed off, his dark eyes troubled. Confused more than troubled, actually. There was no telling what Uncle Robert had led him to believe.

She set her jaw. Why her uncle was so keen to have her marry all of a sudden was beyond her. Clearly he had not believed her earlier in the summer when she had told him she was content to serve as her Aunt Margaret's companion and remain a spinster, no matter how society viewed her choice. Old and dried up at that age of four-and-twenty, according to the *ton*. Which was ridiculous. She was perfectly moisturized and plenty young, thank you very much.

And she *had* been happy, all the way up until about three minutes ago. Now she had an affronted, would-be suitor gaping at her as if she'd, well, rejected his offer of marriage. Sighing, she offered an apologetic smile. "Please know how flattered I am by your proposal. I wish you nothing but the very best in the future, my lord."

The situation could not have been any more awkward. Spending the rest of the week with him was going to be excruciating. Spending the rest of the week with Uncle Robert would be even worse.

She swallowed; she couldn't even think about that now.

As his face grew increasingly mottled, Kensington tugged on the hem of his mustard-colored jacket. "If you'll excuse me, Miss Abbington." The words were stilted and brusque, understandably.

As far as she was concerned, the sooner this interview was over, the better. "Yes, of course," she murmured, dipping into a shallow curtsey. He turned and stalked away, cutting a straight line through the grass toward the house. Expelling a lungful of air, Eleanor sagged against one of the folly's rounded stone columns.

That was an experience she hoped never to repeat.

If he'd only listened to her in the first place. Must people look upon her unmarried status as something to be pitied or remedied? Before her father had died, she had seen all too well the life of a married woman. *That* was something to be pitied—not her perfectly lovely life. Besides attending to Aunt Margaret's comforts, no one ever told Eleanor what to do, how to act, or what to say. No one ever humiliated her, laid a hand on her, or made her cry.

She was free, and she intended to stay that way.

A quarter of an hour later, Eleanor let herself into the empty library, carefully pulling the glass door closed behind her. The cool interior felt good against her flushed cheeks, and she went straight to the nearest chair and collapsed in it. If she were very, very lucky, perhaps no one noticed her coming back to the house. She wasn't ready to face her uncle just yet. She wanted a chance to think of what to say—

Bam!

The door banged open, startling her into sitting up straight. Uncle Robert stalked into the room, his heavy grey brows lowered over narrowed eyes. With his full grey beard and patrician nose, he was only a toga away from looking like a vengeful Zeus.

So much for having time to gather her thoughts.

"For God's sake, Eleanor, have you lost your mind? What would possess you to turn down the suit of such an advantageous match?"

Advantageous? For whom, exactly? Indignation flared to life, trumping her apprehension. Her own brows pinched as she lifted her chin. "I am sorry, Uncle, but I did make it quite clear I had no intentions of marrying Lord Kensington."

"And I made it abundantly clear that Kensington is a valuable political ally with whom I wish to align myself."

"I'm certain he is a fine politician. I am less certain, however, as to his suitability as a husband." The very thought made her stomach ache.

"He's a suitable husband *because* of his politics," he snapped, coming to stand directly in front of her. "This isn't some fairytale, Eleanor. Marriage is a vehicle for strengthening bonds between allies, as you well know."

How could she forget? In the three months since she had come out of half-mourning, he had spoken of little else. Eleanor drew a calming breath, trying to sound rational. "I can appreciate that. However, I am not prepared to sacrifice my entire life so that Lord Kensington feels obligated to vote more favorably. The politics should stand on their own merits, should they not?"

His nostrils flared, though the rest of him remained unnervingly still. "You have no idea of what you speak, and quite frankly, you are far too old for this sort of selfish childishness. Thank God my sister is not around to see the sort of ungrateful person you have become."

His words pierced her armor like a well-placed blade. He knew exactly how to flay her, leaving her breathless. "I will not believe Mama would have wanted me to suffer the same fate as she." Her words were raspy, filled with barely leashed emotion.

The muscles of his jaw hardened, same as his eyes. "And what fate was that? To become a respected member of society? To have children and be the mistress of a great house? To attend the most exclusive balls and dine at the Prince Regent's own table? You should be so lucky to 'suffer' a fate such as hers."

She swallowed hard against the need to lash out. To baldly state the truth they all knew but no one ever said. Antagonizing her uncle at this point would only make things worse. Straightening her spine, she nodded. "I am sorry I have failed your expectations, Uncle. It was never my intention to disappoint you or this family."

He shook his head, regarding her as one might a convicted horse thief. "You've gone too far this time, Eleanor. Your streak of independence must be nipped in the bud. You have a duty to this family, as do I."

She bit her tongue, literally, and nodded. When he set his teeth like that, she knew from past experience it was best simply to agree—no matter how idiotic the statement. So long as she didn't anger him before she left, she could stay out of sight until he cooled down, and he'd likely forget it.

Maybe.

He did look particularly agitated this time.

Linking his hands behind his back he circled her, his pace slow and deliberate. "As the head of this family, I am responsible for the wellbeing and future of each and every one of us. And it's a good thing, since you have so clearly demonstrated you haven't the sense God gave you."

Her head stilled, unable to bob in agreement to this particular statement. How dare he say such a thing to her? A dozen arguments sprang to mind, but she steadfastly clamped her mouth shut. She mustn't fight with him. He was puffing up like a riled cat, and she didn't want to feel the sting of drawn claws.

"Whether you like it or not, Eleanor, it is past time for you to apply yourself to finding a husband. We should have done so the moment you were out of half-mourning. We are fast approaching the time you will be viewed as unsuitable for marriage, rendering yourself useless to this family.

"You've ruined our chances with Kensington. He

has already announced his intention to leave." He made no effort to hide his resentment, pinning her with his furious gaze. "Fortunately, there are three other suitable candidates for marriage who shall be attending the party. Therefore, I have a proposal for you."

He turned to her, waiting for her to acknowledge the statement. He loved to do this—forcing her to bow to his will. Lifting her chin, she said, "Oh?"

"I had thought to announce your betrothal at the welcome dinner tomorrow night, but obviously that won't be the case. However, a betrothal announcement *will* be made by the end of the party. The choice is yours: Lord Henry, Lord Netherby, or Lord Shevington."

Anger coursed through her, turning her blood cold. He couldn't demand such a thing—it was absurd! "Surely you can't be serious. Please, be reasonable, Uncle." Her tone was remarkably composed, thank goodness, despite the fury that had her digging her fingernails into her palms.

"You dare speak of being reasonable to me? After denying Kensington's suit?" Indignation stiffened his shoulders. "I'll have no more of your stubbornness. You will choose a husband who will strengthen this family's future, or I will do it for you."

Her lungs couldn't seem to remember how to function. Her breath came in short, inadequate bursts, starving her of the air she so desperately needed to clear her mind. "And if I refuse?"

He smiled for the first time since entering the room. "Then I suppose I'll have to summon your sister home from Hollingsworth. She's always been so delightfully biddable."

Eleanor's breath left her body in a whoosh. He wouldn't. Libby was barely seventeen—months still from her first Season! Surely he wouldn't force her into marriage with some dry, aged member of parliament who was two or even three times her age merely to secure a favorable vote for his proposed bill.

Surely nothing. The icy blue steel of his gaze plainly told her the truth of his warning. He was dead serious.

Her first instinct was to lash out, to tell him exactly what he could do with his threats. But she couldn't. To do so would only make things worse. She needed time to think, and that meant she had to have him think she would bow to him and his dreadful demand. "I see." Her throat was tight, her words strained. She swallowed and tried again. "If you'll excuse me, it would seem I have much to prepare for in the coming days."

Smug satisfaction lifted the corners of Uncle Robert's full lips. "Excellent."

She couldn't escape the room fast enough. Holding her expression neutral until she made it out of his sight, she dashed down the corridor, heading for the massive staircase that led to her bedchamber. Tears of frustration burned at the back of her eyes, but she refused to let them spill over. She would *not* fall to pieces at another of Uncle Robert's demands.

She finally made it to the entrance hall and was only steps away from escape when the front door opened. *Please, please don't let it be Kensington!* She was not in the state of mind to greet anyone, but most especially not him.

Tolbert, uncle's butler, stepped inside, and her shoulders wilted with relief. But of course she couldn't be that lucky. As the servant stepped aside, the silhouette of a tall, broad-shouldered man came into view.

She blinked. *Definitely* not Lord Kensington. The bright sunshine behind the man hid his face, but she could make out close-cropped hair and an exceedingly fine figure. His upper body, encased in a tightly fitting jacket, narrowed from those wide shoulders down to a

16

lean waist.

For half a second, her distress eased as curiosity flared. Who was this ma—

Oh Lord. It couldn't be.

"Well, well, look who's come to greet this weary soldier. Your dedication truly warms the heart, coz."

"Nicolas?" She gasped. He looked so different—if it weren't for the insolence of his tone, she wouldn't have recognized him at all.

He had always been such a scrawny boy, and had never really changed much as an adolescent, save for his growing taller. He'd only been gone two years. Was it possible to double one's weight in that amount of time? His arms, once thin and lanky, were now padded with muscle, visible even through the fabric of his crimson coat, while his ivory breeches did little to hide his long and powerful legs.

She gave her head a little shake. None of that mattered, for heaven's sake. This was Nick, and as was his talent, he had shown up at the worst possible time. "What are *you* doing here?"

He set his satchel on the tiled floor and handed over his gloves and hat before offering a careless little grin. "I knew how much you must miss me, so when I had the opportunity to come home three weeks early, I jumped at the chance. Oh, I know Mama will be thrilled, but I'm sure that's nothing compared to the delight wending its way through your pitter-pattering little heart at the very sight of me."

"That's *dread*, Nick. I know they start with the same letter, but I'm certain you can tell the difference if you apply yourself."

"No, no—your face says it all. You're beside yourself with joy." He stepped toward her, spreading his arms wide. "Come now, give us a kiss." He puckered his lips like a particularly surprised fish and leaned toward her. It was the same annoying greeting he always gave her, loving as he did to remind her of their first meeting. Having this small bit of normalcy after such a terrible day was oddly comforting.

Rolling her eyes, she put a hand against his chest, blocking his advance. Good heavens, was he hiding a metal breastplate beneath his shirt? She gritted her teeth and blew out a breath. Surely she only noticed these things about him because she was so frazzled from her encounter with her uncle. "I am *not* in the mood, Nicolas."

He angled his head, his gaze far too observant for

her peace of mind. "Shall we proceed directly to the joyful weeping, then? I do believe your eyes are dewy already. Yes, I know, two years is simply too long to do without my company."

Eleanor stiffened under his scrutiny. Yes, her eyes were a little teary, but it had absolutely nothing to do with him. She yanked her hand away and backed up a few steps. "I'm very happy you are alive, intact, and returned to the bosom of your family. Now, if you'll excuse me."

Before she could flee up the stairs, he reached out and snagged her arm. "Elle, is everything . . . all right?" His ever-present grin slipped and for the first time, she could see him for the officer he was.

Blast it, now the tears were threatening all over again. This was Nick; he hadn't a compassionate bone in his body. They teased, mocked, and riled each other, but they didn't do...*this*, whatever this was. She swallowed past the lump in her throat and nodded briskly. "Yes, of course. I'll see you at supper, I'm sure."

He didn't try to stop her when she pulled away, and she dashed up the stairs, not daring to look back. With the mess Uncle Robert had just dumped in her lap, dealing with her annoying cousin was the last thing she needed to worry about.

No matter what strange feelings the sight of him had roused.

Chapter Two

*F*isting his hand at his side, Nick watched as Eleanor fled up the stairs, clutching handfuls of her skirts as she rushed to escape him. His heart pounded like a battle drum despite the brevity of the encounter.

He'd waited so long to see her, and even in her plain white gown and simple coiled braid holding her straight dark hair in check, she still looked better than he remembered.

And he remembered her looking pretty damn good.

He took a long, deep breath. Not exactly the best homecoming in the world. He had always been a burr beneath her saddle, but she'd been particularly agitated, especially considering how long he'd been gone. Something was definitely bothering her, and for once, it wasn't him.

Yes, they rarely shared a civil word, but it was never with any real heat. It was a challenge of sorts to see who could trump the other's barbs most effectively. He learned early on it was the most effective way to engage her, and over the years it had become the norm.

Her scent still lingered in the air, a delicate mix of lavender and honey, the same blend that haunted his dreams. He certainly couldn't do anything now, but perhaps he could wheedle the problem out of her at dinner. Besides, it was a long ride here, and he very much needed a change of clothes and a hearty drink.

He had made the trip from London in record time, pushing Caesar, and later a rented mount, much harder than he should have, but unable to force himself to pull back on the reins. It had been too long, and he had seen too much, to want to delay his homecoming even another minute.

Footsteps in the corridor leading to the west wing jarred him from his woolgathering, and he unfurled his hand and straightened his spine. His stepfather emerged, his gaze already assessing as he approached.

Exactly the person Nick didn't wish to see.

"Malcolm," he said in neutral greeting, offering a slight nod. "I hope you are well." Or not. Either would be fine with him.

"More or less. You're early." It was more accusation than observation.

"Indeed. My plans changed, so I thought I would surprise my mother with my illustrious presence." He heartily wished she was here now, but Tolbert had informed him Mother was visiting the village for the rest of the afternoon.

"Yes, well, try to make yourself presentable before she returns. You could pass for a highwayman in those filthy clothes."

Because no one else on earth would possibly gather a speck of dust on them after a pounding eight-hour journey. "Didn't you know? That's the fashion these days." He grinned simply because he knew it would irk his stepfather.

And it did.

The earl set his jaw, narrowing his eyes for a brief moment. "And here I thought the military would be able to make a man of you."

He always had gone straight for the throat. Good thing Nick had a lifetime of acclimation to such comments. "Well, if you couldn't, what hope did the army have?"

Malcolm's gaze would have frozen lava. "Clearly none. Some people are beyond hope." Without another word, he strode from the room and out the front door.

Evidently nothing had changed.

Relaxing the tense muscles of his shoulders, Nick shook his head. It was ironic, really. During the past few years, Nick had had the meaning of respect drilled into him. As a commissioned officer, he'd been taught to earn the respect of his men, as well as possess a healthy dose of it for his own superiors. But apparently, he still had a blind spot when it came to his stepfather, who incidentally had paid for Nick's commission. Not that he felt bad about it, since clearly the feeling was mutual.

The lofty Earl of Malcolm had never quite forgiven Nick for being part of the package that was his mother. Raising—no matter how loosely such a word could be applied to their situation—another man's orphan wasn't quite what he had in mind when Nick's mother had ensnared the earl all those years ago.

The purposeful clearing of a throat had him looking over to Tolbert. He'd completely forgotten the man was even there. "Yes?"

"Shall I have your room readied, sir?"

There was no missing the censure in old Tolbert's

tone. Fantastic—Nick's arrival had upset yet another member of the household. The butler hated surprises just about as much as he hated laughter, gossip, and puppies. All of which led to the disruption of his schedule, which was worse than any cardinal sin.

Nick nodded, infusing a healthy dose of humility into his expression. "Please, though if it is too much to ask, I am quite adept at making do. I've even slept on God's own dirt a time or two in the not so distant past."

Such a thing would seem the worst possible fate to Tolbert, but in truth, those nights hadn't bothered Nick. When surrounded by people who respected him, even the worst conditions were preferable to this house and its self-important master . . . except for when Eleanor was in residence, of course.

The butler's stiff brow relaxed slightly. "I'm certain we can find something more comfortable than that, sir."

Well, well—was that a bit of dry humor he heard? "So glad to hear it."

"And may I be so bold as to say, welcome home, sir."

His first genuine greeting. Nick smiled and nodded his acceptance. After a distressed cousin and a contentious stepfather, he'd happily take a kind butler right about then. With a sigh, he retrieved his satchel and trudged up the stairs to the rooms he'd so infrequently used these past five or so years.

So far his homecoming was going bloody brilliantly.

***

Step one: discover a large cache of money.

Step two: Purchase a cottage beside the sea.

Step three: Tell uncle to go to the devil.

A perfectly reasonable plan, as far as Eleanor was concerned. There was only one problem: she was fairly certain no undiscovered treasure troves languished on the estate's grounds.

It just seemed so hopeless. She had been unable to come up with any real plan in the two hours since her uncle laid down his ultimatum. It was incredibly frustrating to know he held all the cards. As he well knew, Eleanor would do anything to protect her sweet sister.

Libby had an innocence about her that Eleanor was determined to preserve. Papa had died before she was old enough to recognize the tension in their home, or at the very least to place its origin. She had a rosy view of love and life that would be crushed by some overbearing aristocrat. It was a fate she did not deserve.

Of course, it was a fate Eleanor didn't deserve, either. The whole situation was just so blasted unfair. Blowing out a breath, she paced the length of the room. Aunt Margaret's snores filtered past the ebony door that separated their suites, and Eleanor immediately quieted her footsteps. Her aunt's noise may not wake her, but the woman heard just about everything else in a half-mile radius.

Eleanor would love nothing more than to pour out her frustrations to her aunt, but she had just been so delicate since Mama's death. Gone was the fiery woman who had once been a *tour de force* among the *ton.* Growing up, Eleanor had wanted to be just like her. Widowed young and without children of her own, she had always been so strong and independent—a striking foil to Eleanor's mother while Papa was still alive.

Now, however, she was simply the aging, older sister to one sibling who was dead, and another who was a boorish nobleman who liked to manipulate them about like chess pieces.

And on top of everything, Aunt Margaret had been under the weather this week, and Eleanor didn't want to cause her undue stress. Sighing, she rubbed a hand over her eyes. She wasn't getting anywhere.

A light tap on the door to the corridor interrupted her thoughts. She padded over and pulled it open, only to find Nick on the other side. What on earth was he doing here? His short, brown hair was damp and in need of a comb, standing up in all different directions. He'd taken the time to shave as well, and the late afternoon light illuminated one perfectly smooth, chiseled cheek while the other was cast in shadow.

For one fleeting moment, she had the oddest desire to run a fingertip down the side of his face, to see if the skin was as soft as it looked. And then her sanity returned with a biting snap.

Was he mad? One couldn't go knocking on a woman's bedchamber on a whim. She pulled the door mostly closed, leaving only enough room for him to have a clear view of her censure. "Nicolas," she hissed, annoyance making the single word into a curse, "what are you doing here?"

He lifted one corner of his mouth is a rakish grin, knowing full well that she hated when he acted as though he was some sort of Corinthian. "You ran away without a proper greeting, young lady. I thought I might give you the chance to grovel for my forgiveness before dinner."

"Oh please, I am not a young anything to you. Now go away, I'll see you downstairs soon enough." She started to shut the door, but he put his hand out, stopping her forward motion with a jolt.

"Not until you tell me what is bothering you," he said, an underlying hint of concern coloring the otherwise belligerent words. Then, just when she was about to think he might actually care, he added, "You are not nearly waspish enough for all to be well."

She rolled her eyes, her gaze landing on the bulge of his arm muscles as he held the door in place, resisting her attempts to shut it. It was so jarring for him to look so different. And distracting. Her heart gave a little flip as her gaze slipped over his broadened shoulders and the exceptionally sharp line of his jaw. Truly, they must have worked him like a mule in the army.

Good.

Having regained her wits, she glared at him. "Would you please leave me be?"

"Of course."

"Thank you," she said, exasperation clear in her whispered words.

"Right after you tell me what has your face drawn tight as a miser's purse strings." He gave another infuriating little grin. "Careful, such a thing will give you wrinkles. Especially at your advanced age."

"Oh, do be quiet," she said, shaking her head. "Honestly, Aunt Margaret will hear you, and if you wake her, I *will* make you regret it."

He leaned in toward her until his face was only inches from hers, the clean scent of his shaving soap teasing her nose. His light green eyes held the same challenge they always did when he'd set his mind to having his way. "Then I suggest," he murmured, his voice low and deep, "that you let me in and tell me what is troubling you."

"*You* are troubling me," she insisted, keeping her own voice down. "Now leave. I'll see you at dinner."

Nick sighed, shaking his head as though profoundly disappointed. "Only two years away, and they've turned you into such an old maid."

An *old maid*? For heaven's sake, was everyone intent on labeling her the doddering old woman today? It didn't help that he looked as vibrant and virile as a prize stallion. And to think she had been inadvertently admiring him. The men in her family could go to the devil, as far as she was concerned. Fresh anger welled up from the conversation with Uncle Robert, from the helplessness and impotence of being played like some puppet.

Eleanor jerked the door open so suddenly that Nick stumbled forward, very nearly falling flat on his face. She waited until he recovered to pin him with a frosty glare. "I am *not* an old maid, Nicolas Norton, and *you* are not some sort of confidant. Why would I tell you anything? You've been back all of two hours, and already you have reverted to the wayward young boy who always tagged behind me like a puppy, making trouble for me at every turn."

She would never in a thousand years say such harsh things to any other person on earth, but Nick had always thrived on annoying her. This was what they did. She doubted she would know what to do if he ever offered her a genuine kind word. To do so would mean that he actually took something seriously.

"What is life without a little trouble?" he asked, brushing off her insults. "You know what I think? I think you've missed me."

"Yes, about as much as one misses a hangnail."

He chuckled, his green eyes sparkling despite the

waning evening light. "You do say the sweetest things, Ellie. Lucky for you, I know exactly what you need."

She crossed her arms, looking at him with patent disbelief. He knew nothing about what she needed, nothing at all. She needed freedom, respect, the ability to *not* be married off to the man of Uncle Robert's choosing. "Oh? And what is that, exactly?"

"To meet me at the ruins. Tomorrow at dawn." He gave her a quick wink, made a military turn, and marched from the room.

She blinked, caught off guard. Then a slow, reluctant smile softened the corners of her mouth. For once, he was absolutely right. Devil take the man for knowing her so well.

***

"My, but you are looking *so* well, darling." Nick's mother stretched her lips in a lazy smile from across the dinner table. She was the only person he knew that could manage such an expression without betraying a single wrinkle. Perhaps the vast quantities of drink she had consumed all these years—including tonight—were successfully preserving her after all. "Eleanor, isn't he looking well?"

Ignoring his mother's slightly slurred words, Nick raised an eyebrow at Eleanor, challenging her to disagree with the assessment. He could practically hear her grit her teeth.

"Indeed," she murmured, clearly pained to admit it. An actual compliment would probably kill her.

Although, to be fair, he never complimented her, either. She was slender and beautiful, with full lips that begged to be kissed and gorgeous dark hair that looked so silky, he'd spent the last decade fighting the desire to run his hands through it. All of this, however, would never leave his lips.

Lifting his glass in a mock salute, he said, "Please, cousin, you'll give me a big head with such eager praise."

"You don't need me for that."

"Now, now, the both of you. Do behave at the dinner table." Mother paused to take another drink of her wine before turning her less than focused gaze on Nick. "It's been so long, my son. Please, tell us all about your life in the militia."

Malcolm's knife screeched against porcelain as he cut his roast lamb with much more force than necessary. "I don't think we need to hear about his battlefield experiences, Lavinia."

Nick ran his tongue along his teeth in an attempt to hold back his retort, but it was no use. "Are you certain? I was under the impression gory battlefield details were appropriate conversation for the dinner table, and was about to proceed accordingly."

His stepfather glared daggers above the floral centerpiece as the candlelight flickered menacingly in his eyes.

"Oh, Nicolas, how you tease," Mother trilled. "It's a shame Margaret couldn't join us. She does so enjoy your cheek."

Malcolm's gaze flickered to his wife before returning to his meal. "You remember to keep your *cheek* in hand, Nicolas, while you are in my home."

My home. It was a theme that never quite went away. When he first came to live here fifteen years ago, the man went out of his way to put Nick in his place. As soon as he found a school that would take him, Malcolm packed him off with ill-concealed pleasure and washed his hands of him. If it weren't for school breaks, Nick might have never seen his family.

"That goes for you as well, Eleanor," Malcolm added, residual sharpness hardening his words.

Eleanor's head jerked up at the mention of her name, her forkful of potatoes halted halfway to her mouth. She looked as though she wanted to argue with the unfair admonishment, but instead merely pressed her lips together and nodded.

Damn it—Nick hated to see her like this. Where was her spunk? Her fire? It was as if all the fight in her fizzled whenever the earl so much as glanced at her. Hopefully tomorrow Nick could shake loose the bee in her bonnet.

Mother took a hardy sip from her wine, seeming oblivious to Eleanor's distress. Setting down the goblet, she turned to Malcolm. "How wonderful that Nicolas should be here for the house party, don't you think? I imagine he shall catch quite a few ladies' attention."

Nick could tell exactly how excited his stepfather was with his presence. A firing squad might have been more welcome. "I'd rather he'd have come when he said he would. This party is hardly the place for him."

She pursed her lips, looking as though she were thinking very hard. "Actually, he's come at just the right time. Lord Kensington's absence would have had us in quite the pickle. Now there's no need to fret over our numbers."

Mother's statement had exactly the opposite effect on the mood than Nick would have expected. Malcolm slammed his silverware to the table and snatched up his wine glass. Eleanor jumped at the noise, nearly dropping her fork.

What the hell was going on here? And why had Kensington left before the party had even started? Nick wanted answers, but he'd be damned if he'd ask them with his stepfather around.

Mother, as was usual, was completely unperturbed. "Nicky, darling, I have just the girl for you to entertain. Mr. Landon's oldest daughter turned eighteen this month, and this is to be her first foray into society. She'll officially debut with Libby next Season."

"Just what we need," Malcolm muttered as he set down his drink. "A fresh-faced young debutant providing unfavorable comparison to Eleanor."

Nick very nearly choked on his peas. Of all the . . . he may often tease Eleanor, but Malcolm's comment was designed to draw blood. With outrage burning in his gut, Nick jerked his gaze to her, not even giving a damn if she could sense his fury. Her face was pale, her jaw tight, but she gave her head a quick, nearly imperceptible shake when their eyes met. Her meaning was clear: stay out of it.

Ah hah—he was beginning to realize what might be the cause of her odd behavior since his return. Knowing Malcolm, that was surely not the first comment he had doled out to her as the party approached. Despite her wishes, his fists clenched under the table, a retort poised precariously on his lips.

"Don't worry," Mother said breezily, heedless of the tension at the table. "I'm sure Nicky will have no problem keeping the girl occupied." She smiled broadly, her eyes half closed before lifting her wineglass again and downing the contents.

Glancing once more to Ellie's wane face, Nick finally managed to swallow the words he wanted to say. "Well then," he said, working to keep his tone light, "sounds as though Miss Landon and I should suit perfectly. I'll leave the serious entertaining to Eleanor."

The rigid line of her shoulders relaxed even as her gaze remained fixed on her plate. Malcolm cut his eyes toward her, his gaze hard and steady. "For once, Norton, you may actually be of some use."

Agreement from Malcolm? Something was definitely wrong here. Refusing to break from character, he lifted his glass and tipped his head to his stepfather in a classic arrogant move before taking a long drink.

Whether she wanted to or not, Eleanor *would* tell him what the devil was going on. After all, what good was being trained in the art of war if one couldn't shamelessly exploit it on one's family?

Chapter Three

The swishing of razor thin metal through cool air soothed Eleanor in much the way harp music calmed the music lover, or fine wine pleased the connoisseur. In the early morning gloom, damp fog was her cover, the dim promise of sunrise her only light. She moved forward swiftly, danced backwards, and thrust again. Nothing but mist met her blade, though she couldn't help but imagine her uncle's chest at the end of her buttoned tip.

"Your form is terrible, cousin."

Eleanor gasped at the sudden pronouncement, and swung around, her rapier extended. Nicolas's smiling face was inches from her blade. He didn't even have the decency to flinch, drat the man. "Even my worst form would be miles better than yours."

Leaning back against the crumbing ruins of the old

abbey wall, he nodded solemnly. "I agree wholeheartedly. Unless, of course, we are speaking of fencing. If that is the case, allow me to clear up your misconceptions."

She didn't relax. The way she was feeling this morning, she could happily take her meddling step-cousin's head right off. "Sounds like a challenge to me. Have you come prepared?"

Though they used to meet frequently for these clandestine matches, it had been over two years since their last one. As much as he was a thorn in her side, she would be forever grateful to him for teaching her the sport. It had started as a lark, but had quickly evolved to their favorite form of communication, taking their verbal sparring and converting it into proper duels.

Stepping back, he whipped his own sword up to clang against hers, making an X of the two weapons. "But of course. I wouldn't dare meet anyone at dawn unarmed, least of all you, dear Ellie."

She rolled her eyes, sending a brief glance heavenward before meeting his gaze. His *amused* gaze. Of course. Everything was a game to him.

"*En guard*," she commanded, planting her feet more firmly and extending her left hand behind her for balance. "And *don't* call me Ellie."

"As you wish, my sweet." He paused for a moment, pursing his lips, then backed up a step. "By the way, I'm very sorry about your mother. I know I said as much in my letter, but it was a damn shame."

She blinked, taken aback by his quiet words. *Sincere* words. Leave it to Nick to throw her off kilter. She swallowed against the sadness that rose from deep within her, letting her gaze fall to the rocky ground. "Thank you," she said, nodding twice before looking back up. "I'm very glad to have Aunt Margaret, at least."

She smiled tightly, willing him to move on from the topic. This gentle side of him she kept catching glimpses of unnerved her. She didn't quite know what to make of the changes she saw in him.

As if sensing her desire, he repositioned his blade, tapping it lightly against hers. "Shall we?"

"Do you think you can keep up?" she asked, lifting a brow in challenge.

Below his morning scruff, his lips curled in his signature grin. She let out a relieved breath—they were back on familiar ground. He knew it drove her mad when he gave her that self-satisfied smile, which meant he was rarely without it. "Now, do try to be nice. It's been weeks since I've had a proper match."

Before the last word had even left his mouth, she lunged forward, going straight for his gut. He flitted backwards, parrying her move and striking forward with one of his own. His foil slapped against her right shoulder.

She gritted her teeth, not so much against the sting of the hit as the sting to her pride. He was toying with her, damn him. "Two years in the militia and *that's* all you've got?" She tsked as they both got back into position. After the awfulness that was last night's dinner, this was exactly what she needed.

"Taking it easy on an old gal like you."

"Old gal? I'm all of two years older than you, thank you very much." She engaged him once more, darting forth with lightning speed and poking his ribs with a sound thump.

"Ow," he laughed, slapping her foil away with his own. "Careful, that's tender young flesh. You've likely forgotten how delicate youthful skin can be."

She bit her bottom lip to keep from grinning. He was always such a pest. For that little quip, he earned himself a slap across his gloved hand. "Sorry, did that hurt? You're right; I can hardly remember what such a hit feels like. Though it's less from my advanced age and more from the lack of a proper opponent."

"Ah, you've missed me. Should I come home more often then? Clearly you are in want of my company if it is a proper opponent you seek."

He whipped his foil up again and charged her, a move that she easily deflected. They carried on for a few more swings, the clashing of their blades ringing out in the pre-dawn hush. She was starting to enjoy herself, to push aside the fury of her recent arguments with Uncle Robert, and give herself over to the mind game that was fencing.

When she finally had the upper hand, she tagged Nick once more on the shoulder. "Ha! What were you saying about a proper opponent? Unless your valet cares to extend his services, I know not why your visiting home more often should make a difference in my ability to find a worthy adversary."

He shook his arm out, but still smiled that maddening grin of his. "It's a pity you've had to make do without an opponent in my absence. I'm sure Aunt Margaret and Malcolm would be happy to help you find one, should they learn of your early morning exercise."

She knew very well he was teasing, but still she

lifted her tip toward his neck. "You wouldn't dare say a word, since you are the sole reason I have taken to fencing. Feeble-minded female that I am, I was easily led astray by my dear, trusted cousin."

He snorted, stepping back at the same moment to deflect her foil. "If you're feeble-minded, then I'm a weakling. And we both know that's not true," he said, purposely bullying his way toward her with hard, fast slashes of his blade.

Not true, indeed. Even as she concentrated on defending herself, her gaze darted toward him of its own volition, catching glimpses of his hardened chest through his loose, open-necked shirt. His sleeves covered muscled forearms that she knew would be flexing this way and that, and his biceps strained against the fabric despite its generous cut. Awareness washed over her, peppering her skin with goose bumps. Good heavens, he must be as strong as an ox now.

She bit her lip, forcing her mind back to their volleys, both verbal and physical. "You know Uncle Robert would never believe otherwise." Her words came out in staccato puffs as she struggled to hold her ground.

"Because the man's an idiot."

The comment caught her off guard, making her

grin. He immediately took advantage, surging forward with a volley that forced her backwards, pinning her against one of the tumbledown half-walls that once delineated the abbey's courtyard. Drat it all—how had he gotten the upper hand so quickly? Her breath came out in a rush as he leaned against her; the X of their crossed foils the only thing preventing his chest from pressing against hers. She went a little lightheaded at the thought.

The crisp scent of sweat and soap surrounded her as his lips lifted in a slow, smug smile. "You've gone soft," he murmured, shaking his head. "That was entirely too easy."

Oh, no—there was no way on earth she would allow him to win this, their first battle in so long. Especially when her whole body seemed to be betraying her. Her nerves tingled at his closeness, her lungs willfully drawing in the scent of him. Forcing herself to relax, she offered a contrite smile. "I suppose I'm out of practice. Take your pound of flesh and be done with it."

She turned her cheek, waiting for him to lean forward for the kiss he had long claimed as his prize of choice. Just another way to remind her of how he had bested her in their first meeting.

He bent forward, his green eyes alight with mischief. She held her breath, working to maintain the focus that wavered at his nearness. Just when she was about to spring, at the very moment her muscles tensed to counter attack, he stopped, tsking. "If you think," he said quietly, his lips only inches from her flushed cheek, "that I would believe for a second you would just roll over and let me win, you have underestimated me, cousin."

Smarter than she had hoped. Fighting to regain her flagging resolve in the face of his overwhelming closeness, she shrugged. "Then prepare yourself."

With every ounce of her strength, she launched herself on the offensive, forcing him away and whipping her foil up between them.

He mirrored her position, his hand held out behind him with his legs evenly planted on the rocky ground. "See? Not feeble-minded in the least. Stubborn, willful, and scandalous, but never feeble-minded."

They engaged once more, the clanging of their swords carrying across the dew-laden field. "I am not scandalous, thank you very much."

He blocked her jab and countered with one of his own, but she saw it coming and danced back just in time.

"But stubborn and willful?"

She smiled. "A woman never argues with a compliment."

Chuckling, he dodged her strike and repositioned himself. "That explains so very much."

"Good. And a woman unwed is not scandalous. She is *independent*." The fierceness with which she said the words felt good. The match was helping to give her back a bit of her confidence. Being with him somehow made her feel stronger.

He widened his eyes dramatically, gasping in mock disbelief. "Independence is *so* much worse than scandal. Malcolm would be in vapors to hear you speak thusly."

Standing in the middle of the ruins, dressed in wholly improper clothes and clutching a sword of all things, she couldn't help but laugh. Lowering her foil, she put her free hand to her waist. "Look at me, Nick. I do believe independence would be the least of his objections were he to see me right now."

She hadn't meant it literally, but still his gaze swept over her, taking in her flowing, wide-legged trousers and sturdy, well-fitting long-sleeve blouse made of padded linen. It was impossible to miss the flash of appreciation in his celadon eyes. The oddest tug answered low in her belly, as though gravity had released her for a moment. Or perhaps it was reason leaving her body.

He tipped his head to the side. "Point conceded."

Purposely looking away, she tucked her foil beneath her arm and tugged off her thick gloves. "Speaking of which, it's getting late. I'd best get back before I'm missed."

"Too late."

She frowned, glancing to the first pink fingers of dawn stretching into the sky, heralding the start of the day. "Not at all. I have a good quarter hour before sunrise."

Leaning his sword against the abbey wall, he stepped toward her, shaking his head. "No, I don't mean you *will* be missed. I mean you *have* been missed."

Her heart skittered as he extended his hand to her. Why was she acting such the fool around him? He was treating her exactly as he always had—since they were children, in fact—yet everything seemed to hold a different meaning. She was reacting to him as though he hadn't spent the first decade of their acquaintance driving her mad.

When she didn't move, he gave a one-shouldered shrug. "You'd be amazed what you'll miss when your only companions are a few hundred under-washed, stir crazy soldiers."

Resolutely, she shoved aside the strange feelings, and accepted his proffered hand. "Yes, well, I suppose I may have missed you as well. You do serve as quite the magnet for Uncle Robert's temper, which I inadvertently benefit from. At the very least, I'm glad you didn't get yourself killed on some Godforsaken battlefield."

"Careful cousin—a man can begin to think you actually care for him, with such gushing concern." He winked before tugging her into an easy, one-armed embrace. The hard wall of muscled side was a far, far cry from the slim, lanky build she always associated with him. With his free hand, he gripped her chin in a firm hold and planted a loud, smacking kiss on her cheek.

To her shock, heat seared her skin, and she had to force herself to breathe normally. Still, she did exactly what she always had, making a show of scrubbing at her cheek with her sleeve, wrinkling her nose in disgust. "Ugh—must you insist on accosting me?"

Her tone was as light as always, his expression every bit as teasing. It was a scene they had engaged in for years. So why, oh why did she feel as though she was meeting him for the first time?

"Off you go, Ellie. No sense risking trouble merely to bask in the glory of my company a few moments longer."

She'd do very well to remember that.

Chapter Four

*W*hen Nick had pushed himself in his bid to make it home as soon as possible, it most certainly was not so he could find himself stuck in the midst of a house party. Yet, as he scanned the twenty or so guests mingling beneath the glittering chandeliers of the Manor's impressive drawing room, he resigned himself to exactly that fate.

He cut his gaze to where Eleanor stood beside Malcolm, a smile fixed on her full lips as she greeted Lord Netherby. The man had gained at least two stone since the last time Nick had seen him, though apparently he was still attempting to fit into the same clothes. His expression was that of one inspecting a horse at Tattersall's as his eyes freely roamed Eleanor's figure.

Lecherous old codger. Would it be bad form to grab

the man by his too-small jacket and toss him out on his ear? It didn't help that Eleanor had changed into a perfectly fitted white and turquoise gown that suited her coloring just so. Never mind the other young women peppering the room—she stood out as the Incomparable she was.

She could have easily taken the *ton* by storm, had she decided to do so. Though he hated how she had come about her feelings on matrimony, he was glad for them nonetheless. It was the only thing that kept the jealousy at bay as she turned to greet yet another male guest.

In contrast to her polite but distant facade, Malcolm was thoroughly enjoying himself. Every time he moved on to another guest, he guided Eleanor around like a dog on a lead, his hand firmly grasping her upper arm.

Nick took a sip of wine, continuing his surveillance over the rim of the glass. His stepfather's domineering ways didn't surprise him, but Eleanor's continued passivity did. She hardly looked like the same person he had met at the ruins earlier. In the morning gloom, she had stood straight, tall, and proud. He hated seeing her inner light squelched by Malcolm now. For a moment he considered intervening, but it would probably only serve to annoy her.

"Nicky, darling," his mother said from behind him, "I must introduce you to Miss Landon."

Suppressing a sigh, he turned and nodded to his mother. She was arm in arm with a pretty young blonde girl who smiled up at him with a shy smile.

"Miss Landon, allow me to introduce to you my son, Mr. Nicolas Norton. He is an officer in the militia, and he has only just returned yesterday after an extended absence. We are so thrilled to have him home safe."

Nick bowed as the girl curtsied. "A pleasure to meet you, Miss Landon."

A delicate pink blush touched the apples of her cheeks. "We've met before, Mr. Norton, though I doubt you would remember it. I was but a girl, and you were home from Cambridge for a few weeks."

She looked to be 'but a girl' still, with rounded freckled cheeks and wide blue eyes. Though he would have sworn he didn't know her from Eve, he smiled politely and said, "Well, it is good to see you all grown up."

Mother patted her arm. "I had forgotten all about that. You've some catching up to do, then. Why don't the two of you talk—I see Lord Henry is in want of conversation." With a none-too-subtle wink at Nick, she floated away, waving her fingers at the widowed earl.

"Is this your first house party, then?" Nick asked, struggling to keep his attention on the girl when Eleanor was visible just over her shoulder.

"Indeed, sir." She glanced around the room, surreptitiously taking in the other guests. "I must say, I'm feeling a bit out of place."

"What, you don't normally fraternize with old, yet politically important, men?"

Her cheeks turned scarlet, and she ducked her head. "I can scarce believe you said that," she said, biting her lip against laughter. "I was referring to how very sophisticated everyone is—men *and* women."

He waved his hand dismissively. "Sophisticated is just another word for old and boring. Though I will grant there are a few exceptions here tonight. Not many, but some."

She giggled, covering her mouth with her hand. "Oh, do stop, Mr. Norton. My mother would have my head if she overheard this conversation."

"Ah, but that is the beauty of a house party, Miss Landon. With my mother agreeing to be your chaperone, you are as good as free to do whatever you like."

They both glanced at his mother, who was lifting a wine glass from a passing tray as she stood entirely too close to Henry.

"Regardless, I'm much too terrified of incurring my mother's wrath to make even the smallest *faux pas*. It's a long time until the Season—I'd rather not spend it listening to her lectures on propriety."

"I'd be more worried about impropriety when you are with Nicolas, Miss Landon." Eleanor, apparently having broken free of her jailor, grinned at the girl. "He can be quite the trouble-maker."

"Noted, Miss Abbington," she answered, returning the smile. "Mr. Norton, you must be on your best behavior around me."

Nick offered the pair of them his most rakish look, making Miss Landon giggle and Eleanor roll her eyes.

"It shan't work, Nick. Miss Landon is a friend, and I will not allow her to be fooled into believing you are the consummate gentlemen."

It was a relief to see a spark of mischief glinting in her eyes. He affected his most solemn expression, shaking his head. "Have no fear, Miss Landon. I am a reformed man, courtesy of the army. If Eleanor wasn't so busy playing the part of the social butterfly, she might have noticed what an utterly charming and devoted companion I am tonight. Isn't that so?"

The girl went along with his teasing, nodding. "Yes, utterly.

Eleanor arched a dark eyebrow, "Somehow I'm not convinced. I suppose I shall have to take your very dubious word for it, since I'm much too busy to keep an eye on you this evening."

Spreading his arms, he let a wicked grin turn up the corners of his mouth. "And yet, here you are."

She opened her mouth to respond, but Malcolm interrupted, sidling between Nick and Eleanor. "Pardon me, but I'm afraid I must steal Eleanor away. There are many who wish to speak with you, my dear."

The mere sound of his stepfather's voice put Nick's teeth on edge. Why was he acting as though Eleanor was his to command tonight?

Returning his stepfather's false smile in spades, Nick said, "Yes, including Miss Landon and myself. I'm certain the others will expect her to mingle with everyone present, and we wouldn't want Miss Landon to be neglected."

It was only because he was watching that he caught the flash of surprise in Eleanor's eyes. Before he could interpret whether she was pleased or not by his interference, Eleanor pasted the artificial smile back in place and raised her gaze to meet his. "Uncle Robert's right, I should return to my duties. But it is so lovely to have you with us, Miss Landon. I do hope Nicolas will find it within him to be good company for you."

Nick had to work to keep his expression neutral. What the devil had gotten into her lately? Why was she being so damned biddable? She may look perfectly content to others, but he knew her too well. He could see her strain in the way she held her mouth, and the dullness of her normally luminous brown eyes.

It made him want to shake her, to make her confide in him. Had her mother's death changed her so much, or was it something else?

Pulling Eleanor away from them, Malcolm said, "I'm quite certain Norton can provide all the entertainment Miss Landon could hope for." With a slight bow, he headed for Lord Shevington, pulling Eleanor along with him. Nick couldn't help but be put in mind of a sacrificial lamb.

"Well, that was a bit awkward," Miss Landon said, biting her lip as she looked after Eleanor.

"Indeed," he murmured, narrowing his eyes in

57

thought. Did Malcolm think he could use Ellie as some sort of pawn? He took a good hard look around the room. There were an inordinate number of members of the House of Lords present—several of whom were unmarried. There was no disguising the fact that this house party was meant to strengthen political bonds.

A thought occurred to him, one so distasteful he nearly crushed the stemware in his hand before he realized what he was doing. Did Malcolm have visions of marrying her off to one of these overly dry, mostly older men? Nick had no doubt that if his stepfather couldn't get by on his politics, he'd use whatever weapon he had in his arsenal to get what he wanted.

And Nick would be damned if he'd let Eleanor be the man's ammunition.

***

With a bland smile firmly in place, Eleanor pretended to listen as Lord Shevington droned on about his hunting trip to Scotland last month. She couldn't have cared less about the details of the hunt, but she was determined to appear to Uncle Robert that she was abiding by his ultimatum.

The very thought of his words poisoned her mood,

and she swallowed against the lump that lodged in her throat. It had been over a day since Uncle Robert had thrown down the gauntlet, and absolutely no alternative had presented itself, no matter how much she tried to think of one.

She could refuse, make a fuss, cause a scandal—but all of them seemed to come back to her sister paying the price. Libby deserved a Season, blast it. More than that, she deserved the chance to decide her own future.

By God, Eleanor wouldn't let her uncle steal that from her.

Laughter from across the room caught her attention, and she glanced to where Nick stood with Miss Landon and Lady Blackwell. Her brittle smile softened just a bit. It had been the highlight of her night when he had attempted to free her from her uncle's control.

Or was it just that he enjoyed being contrary to his stepfather? That was more likely the case, but still, she appreciated the effort.

"Don't you agree Miss Abbington?" Shevington blinked at her expectantly, his old-fashioned whiskers making him look like a squirrel begging for a nut.

"Of course," she said with conviction, having no idea to what she was agreeing. Whatever it was, it made the man smile and carry on.

Sneaking a glance in Nicolas's direction again, she was struck with an unexpected pang in the vicinity of her ribs as Miss Landon giggled at something he said. It was the oddest sensation—she'd never once felt jealously where Nick was concerned. He was a pest; surely she was just envious of their freedom. It had nothing to do with the brief touch of Miss Landon's fingers to his sleeve, or the way he tilted his head toward her when he spoke.

Ugh—she *had* to get a hold of herself. This was Nick! The bane of her existence, her competitor, her own personal tag-along tormentor. Clearly Uncle Robert's demands had addled her brain.

Speaking of which, she should be paying more attention to Shevington. A low burn deep in her chest nagged at her, threatening to turn to full-blown panic. The men she had met so far tonight either were old enough be her father, or worse—reminded her of him. Polished manners, polite smiles, but with a certain arrogant authority about them that could easily translate to overt possessiveness or unreasonable rage.

She shuddered, pushing back against the memories that threatened to surface at the thought of her father.

"Are you chilled, Miss Abbington? Shall I have a footman fetch you a wrap?"

Caught in her woolgathering, though thankfully he didn't seem to recognize it as such. She purposefully relaxed her tense shoulders and smiled. "No thank you, my lord. I think perhaps I could use some refreshment."

"Allow me to fetch you something to drink," he replied, bowing his head before lumbering off in search of a servant.

Eleanor breathed a sigh of relief. Finally—a moment of peace. Of their own volition, her eyes strayed once more toward Nicolas. Miss Whittingham had joined them and was fluttering her eyelashes as though caught in a windstorm. Not that Eleanor blamed the girl for trying to flirt with him—he was the youngest man present. And his regimentals did rather stand out among the sea of somber jackets the other men wore.

"Eleanor," Uncle Robert murmured from directly behind her, his hot breath uncomfortably damp against her ear, "I suggest you ignore your little friends and set your focus on the task at hand. Not that I mind choosing a husband for you."

She turned, as much to escape his invasion of her space as anything. "I'm aware of what I should be doing," she said through clenched teeth. At that moment, Shevington returned with a glass in each hand, and she gratefully accepted the one he held out to her.

She was beginning to understand why Aunt Lavinia liked spirits so well.

***

"Did you have a good evening, my dear?" Aunt Margaret, looking better than she had in days, smiled up at Eleanor from the chaise lounge nearest the windows. The drapes had been pulled wide to allow the morning sun to infuse the small, private sitting room they shared.

Eleanor mustered a tired smile as she tucked a blanket more securely around her aunt's legs. "I certainly met a lot of people," she hedged, settling into the chair closest the chaise. It didn't seem particularly good form to respond, "I spoke with none but boring, self-important old men most of the evening, all the while chained to Uncle Robert's side."

The one and only highlight of the night had been just before she'd gone to bed. Nick had caught her on the stairs and murmured, "I do so love a good sunrise, don't you, cousin? I shall enjoy it tomorrow at the start of the hunt, and perhaps the day after that in a more . . . *private* locale."

Of course he could only mean the ruins. After the evening she had endured last night, the idea of pouring out her frustrations through her foil had tremendous appeal. She only wished they could have met this morning. But, with the hunt planned, such a thing would be impossible. At least the men would be gone for most of the morning and she could escape the need to endure the forced match making.

"Interesting, but not an answer to my question," her aunt said, bringing Eleanor back to the conversation at hand. "I have met many people in my day, and not all of them served to enrich an evening."

Eleanor's smile was genuine. "You know me too well. All right, it was a passable evening. I spent most of the time speaking with Uncle Robert's acquaintances."

Her aunt's thin white eyebrows rose, wrinkling her normally smooth forehead. "Heavens, whatever for? A drier group of men I cannot imagine. Were not Miss Landon and Miss Hollister present? Or even Lady Blackwell?"

"Oh, they were. And I was fortunate to have a few moments with each of them. But it was my mission to get to know Lords Henry, Netherby, and Shevington better." A mission enforced relentlessly by Uncle Robert.

Aunt Margaret pursed her lips. "Lords . . . oh, I see. They are all bachelors, are they not?"

Good, she was catching on. "Indeed," Eleanor responded with an ironic grin. She knew her aunt would understand exactly how distasteful such a proposition would have been for her.

Unaccountably, a soft smile brightened her aunt's face. "I'm so very glad to hear it, my dear. Perhaps there is hope for you yet."

Stunned, Eleanor blinked, trying not to show her dismay. *Perhaps there was hope for me yet?* Clearly Aunt Margaret mistook her conspiratorial grin for one of earnestness.

So the truth comes out.

Her heart sank low in her chest, weighed with disappointment and betrayal. Could not *one* of her relatives see that marriage wasn't something Eleanor wanted? She had thought Aunt Margaret understood that, and that she liked having Eleanor around for her companion. In the back of her mind, she had hoped her aunt would raise an eyebrow and say, "How dreadful!" She had imagined confiding in the older woman and having the satisfaction of her gasping in outrage when she heard of her brother's manipulation.

But no—apparently even she wished for Eleanor to drop her objections and marry. Her very soul ached with the knowledge. There truly was no one to champion her.

Oblivious to Eleanor's distress, Aunt Margaret pushed aside the blanket and came to her feet. "I must say, I am feeling much improved this morning. I do believe I shall be fit to join you downstairs today."

Eleanor nodded dully. "I shall inform the countess at once."

It occurred to her as she stood and padded woodenly for the door that only one person had shown her any amount of support in the last few days.

The very last person she would have thought: Nicolas.

***

If ever there was a worthless waste of time and perfectly good lead, it was surely grouse hunting. Nicolas stifled a yawn as he tramped through the underbrush a few yards back from the others. It was all so damned civilized and organized. Everyone walked forward, waited for the flock to be set to air, then shot at the lot of them as if there was any real sport in it. Already the day's take numbered in the hundreds, and beaters were doing their damnedest to flush out stragglers.

Finally, a cluster of birds rose toward the low clouds, and gun after gun discharged. Sighing, he raised his weapon to his shoulder, aimed for a perfectly innocent looking cloud to the left of the flock, and fired.

There. Duty fulfilled. Three hundred birds bagged, twelve gentlemen entertained, and one tedious morning at an end.

"If that's the best the army has to offer, old boy, it's a wonder old Boney ever tasted defeat." Handing over his gun to the servant beside him, Lord Henry laughed and walked over to where Nick stood.

Offering a good natured grin, Nick nodded. "Too right. I suppose it's fortunate that humans are a much larger, less flighty target." He wasn't about to inform the man that he was as good a shot as any man present.

From half the field away, Malcolm's head turned in their direction, his interest in their conversation clear. He quickly shoved his gun to his attendant and scurried over to join them. Scared Nick would say something politically ruinous, was he?

"What an excellent bag, Henry. You must have singlehandedly brought down four dozen birds today."

The man's chest puffed up as though such praise was the highest of possible compliments. "Well, your lands offered quite the bounty. I hope I'll have the opportunity to join you again in the future." He paused and gestured toward Nick. "Perhaps you can give your boy Norton here a lesson or two by then so he can keep up with us."

The two older men shared a laugh, though Malcolm's was harsh and devoid of humor. He was surely stewing at Nick being referred to as his boy. "Sadly, some simply aren't born with a talent for sports—and they're called *women*. What, exactly, is your excuse, Norton?" This brought on fresh laughter, setting Nick's teeth on edge.

Forcing a pleasant smile, he said, "Must have been my pauper father. He spent his days toiling in the courts and had little time for the finer gentlemanly pursuits. By the time Malcolm took me in, I fear it was too late."

It wasn't quite true—his father was a respected barrister who enjoyed the occasional hunting trip. That, however, wouldn't have needled Malcolm nearly as much. In his eyes, Nick's father might as well have been a clerk. Reminding his guests of his stepson's humble origins meant bringing attention to a black smudge on his noble family lineage. Already Nick was reaping the rewards of the comment as his stepfather's eyes narrowed in ill-concealed fury.

Nick grinned. Malcolm could consider it repayment for the way he'd treated Eleanor last night. It little mattered that the man wouldn't realize it. Nick had scored a point against him, and that was good enough for now.

"Damned pity," Henry said, shaking his head as they started back toward the house. "I wonder, is your son a good shot?"

"The best. The boy's a natural."

Lord Henry chuckled, clasping his hands behind his back. "Just like his father. Speaking of your excellent family relations, I do hope I'll have the opportunity to enjoy more time with Miss Abbington. She is quite a lovely young woman."

Nick stiffened, his jaw clenching at the mention of Eleanor. Already she had spent too much of her time with the man. She hadn't looked particularly pleased by it, but she had made no efforts to disengage. He couldn't help the grimace that idea wrought—the man was old enough to be her father!

But as vehemently opposed to the idea as Nick was, Malcolm appeared absolutely delighted. Clasping the earl on the back, he nodded. "Nothing would please me—or her—more."

Chapter Five

"What if I were to seek employment?"

Metal pinged against metal as Eleanor parried Nick's rather sneaky advance-lunge. He was quite nimble for the early hour. Perhaps he too had woken with the burn of anticipation for their match.

He lifted an eyebrow as he retreated, raising his foil once more. "Are there very many opportunities for mediocre female fencers?"

Invigorated by their play, she grinned for the first time that morning, shaking her head. "My, don't we think we're clever. All that overt female attention these past two days must have fooled you into believing you were actually witty, and not just the only man present under the age of thirty."

"And here I thought you liked all those old codgers.

You're certainly spending enough time with them." The grin was in place, but his tone was more biting than usual.

"Yes, because I have *so* much choice in the matter." She saw an opening and took it, executing a perfect raddoppio before thrusting her point into his ribs. It went a long way toward venting her frustration.

Nick grimaced and fell back, rubbing a hand over the wound. "Good hit," he conceded, offering a quick salute of his blade.

"Thank you. And I was thinking of becoming a companion," she said, returning to the point of the conversation. It was wishful thinking; it wasn't as though she could simply leave and take her sister with her.

"Do you think someone would actually pay you to keep them company? I should think they would pay for the opposite." The last word came out on a whoosh of air as he attacked. Their blades carried on the conversation for the moment until he slipped past her defenses and tagged her hip.

Falling back to catch her breath, she finally answered him. "If that worked, you'd be a wealthy man by now."

"*Touche*," he said, chuckling lightly. "I suppose Aunt Margaret might be inclined to pay you, if you should insist."

Fresh disappointment settled on her shoulders and she lowered her foil. "I don't think so. At the moment, she's just as enamored as Uncle Robert at the prospect of marrying me off."

"Don't be silly," he scoffed, his words clipped. "They know as well as I do that you'll not be falling into the parson's trap. Plus there's the issue of finding a man to put up with you," he added, giving her a light, teasing tap beneath her chin with the blunted tip of his blade.

She tensed, hating even speaking of the hopelessness of the situation. "You're wrong. They can't wait to foist me off on the highest bidder."

The teasing light faded from his eyes. "Is that what this tension in the house has been all about? They want for you to marry, despite your wishes?"

She gave a curt nod.

Giving an exaggerated roll of his eyes, he said, "Then tell them to go to the devil and move on. Stop acting like a docile pony and stand up for yourself."

She stiffened. Just who did he think he was? "It's not that easy. And I don't appreciate the analogy."

"Then stop being so damned analogous. Find that elusive thing called a backbone and fight them on this. I know Malcolm. He'll be angry, but it's not as though he'll toss you out on the street, for God's sake. This family doesn't work that way."

She should be so lucky. She'd take that any day over her uncle's true threats. For a moment she considered telling him everything, pouring out the full extent of the turmoil brewing within, but what good would that do? He'd only dismiss her worries, just as he was dismissing them now. "You don't know anything about what he'd do."

"Don't I?" he said, quirking a brow in challenge. "If anyone would be tossed out on the street, don't you think it would be me?"

Where had *that* come from? "What are you talking about?"

He jabbed his blade's point into the earth, resting his hand loosely on the hilt. "A mongrel like me? With no lineage or noble blood to speak of? He'd sooner be cleaved to the plague."

He actually seemed to mean it. Cocky, arrogant, self-satisfied Nick, speaking of himself as though he were a blight on his family? This was uncharted territory for them, this gravity. She honestly didn't know whether to take him seriously or not. "Come now," she said, falling back on their usual banter. "A Frenchman, perhaps, but certainly not the plague."

"Do you have any idea how much money that man has spent in the sole pursuit of keeping me as far from his home as he can manage?" He snorted, shaking his head. "Harrow, Cambridge, even the bloody army. It's a wonder he didn't try to bribe an infantryman to 'accidentally' discharge his weapon in my direction."

Eleanor shifted, unsure of what to say. He seemed genuinely distressed, but knowing him, he was probably just setting her up for some scathingly witty rejoinder. "My, my—who knew you were fit for Drury Lane?"

Extracting his blade, he pointed the buttoned tip of his foil toward her chest. "Right. You're waxing on about being tossed out the window like the contents of a chamber pot, and *I'm* the one being dramatic?"

Her brows came together defensively. Of the two of them, she was by far the most sensible. "I'm *not* being dramatic. And I'm not talking about being tossed out. I'm facing facts."

Letting the weapon fall to his side, he gave her a patently disbelieving look. "And what convoluted 'fact' is that? That Malcolm will actually march you down to the church alter, forcing you to marry or else?"

The very thought made her stomach churn. It was exactly the scenario she feared would happen. "Yes," she ground out.

"Eleanor, this is ridiculous. You don't have to marry." He spoke with such conviction, she almost believed him.

Sometimes, very rarely, a side of him came out that almost made her feel as though he was on her side. Protective of her, even.

"I don't have a choice, Nicolas. Either I choose a husband, or Uncle Robert will do it for me."

***

Nick saw red—and it wasn't just the breaking dawn, which turned the sky a violent crimson. Gripping his foil so tightly his hand ached, he stepped toward her. "He said that?"

She pressed her lips together and nodded. "Right after I turned down Lord Kensington's offer of marriage only days ago."

Bloody hell—Malcolm had gone too far this time. He'd be damned if he let his stepfather get away with this. There was a certain amount of selfishness in his reasons, but more than anything, Nick didn't want Eleanor to be forced into the one thing she feared most. Anger burned in his gut, heating his blood.

"The man's a damn fool."

"That may be the case, but he also is the head of this family." She lifted those big brown eyes up to him, the effect of which was amazingly similar to a kick in the gut. "At least with you he was content to throw money at the problem. His only solution with me is to guarantee ruining my life, no matter which way I choose."

A light breeze tugged at the loosened hair around her face, pulling the raven strands across her too-pale skin. He had the maddest desire to comb the silky strands back with his fingers and kiss her for real. Not the playful kisses he always demanded from her as payment, but a true kiss that would steal her breath and completely override the worry that turned down the edges of her cupid-bow lips.

And he knew exactly how worried she must be. After the way her bastard father had treated her mother, marriage was about as attractive to her as running naked through Mayfair.

"I would never let him ruin your life, Ellie." The words were too charged, too honest. She glanced up sharply and he forced a smile. "Where else could I find another dreadful fencing partner to make me look so good?"

She rolled her eyes. "Very funny. You could hardly influence his choice of tea, let alone what he wants to do with me."

Damn it all—he wished she would have a little faith in him. Yes, he was younger than her, and yes, theirs had been an unconventional relationship, but didn't she realize he would walk through fire for her?

No, of course she didn't, because he would never let her know such a thing. To her, he would always be the inferior, annoying little boy his mother had foisted on the family. A sparing partner, both verbally and otherwise, who provided small entertainment and great annoyance, by her own description.

No, she would see no rescue from him. So he had to do the next best thing: show her that she could save herself. Which from the look of it would be quite the undertaking. She stood there, already defeated, her brow wrinkled with worry as if she had no hope left in her life. That made him even angrier than Malcolm's asinine pronouncement.

Where was his little fighter? Where was the girl who had taken to combat like a bird to the sky, for no other reason than to have it out with him? Dropping back into fighting position, he whipped up his blade. "*En garde*," he demanded.

She stared at him in confusion, her foil still idle at her side. "Nick—"

"*En garde*," he barked again, swishing his weapon through the air in warning.

Warily, she raised her foil and planted her feet. He sprang into action, lunging at full force. She yelped and stumbled backward, glaring at him.

"What was that for?"

He didn't answer. Instead he engaged, forcing her to defend herself or be struck. She didn't disappoint. After a few hits, she started to get angry, her cheeks gaining color and her eyes narrowing in fierce concentration. That's when she really began to fight. The clash of metal against metal rang through the morning air, punctuated by harsh breathing and grunts of exertion. Around them, the red light of dawn grew brighter and brighter, but he had no intention of relenting, not yet.

"What. . . .has . . . gotten . . .into you!" She ground out through clenched teeth as her foil whipped left and right, parrying his attacks.

"Shut up and fight," he growled, punctuating the words with powerful hits. They danced back and forth, their feet moving over the rocky ground almost in unison. Sweat poured down his face and dampened his shirt, but still he didn't let up. He wasn't going to coddle her, damn it. He wanted her to work, to be forced to battle as if their lives depended on it.

As she retreated from his lunge, she stumbled over a rock, falling hard on her backside. "Ow! Nick, wait—!"

But he didn't wait. Dirt flew as she scrambled away from him, abandoning her weapon. Oh no, he wasn't about to let her give up. He kicked the foil back at her, waiting for her to pick it up. Frustration came off her in waves as she reclaimed it and struggled to her feet, sucking in gusts of air. She jerked a hand through her hair, scraping the fallen strands back from her sweaty face.

With a warrior yell, she came at him, her swings even stronger, her precision more deadly. Again and again she jabbed and slapped her blade against him, even tearing his shirt at the shoulder. *This* was more like it. *This* was a woman on fire, damn it. He met her swing for swing, making her work for every small point.

"Getting a little angry, are we?" he said, forcing the arrogant smile he knew she hated.

"*Yes*," she fairly growled, advancing again and again. Finally, she was giving it all she had. She was focused, and driven—furious as a caged lioness—and every bit as glorious as a Greek goddess of war. Her cheeks were red, her eyes flashing. Her body was all that was powerful yet graceful. He'd never seen her so passionate, and he loved it.

Again and again she forced him backward, forced him to yield to her onslaught. As his back smacked against the ruins of the old abbey wall, he jarred to a stop, losing his grip on his weapon. His foil clattered to the ground between them.

For a moment they just stared at each other, their shoulders heaving as they panted for air. And then her eyes grew wide with shock as she realized what this meant. She'd beat him. For the first time ever, she had won. Eleanor pointed her blade directly at his heart, as the certainty of victory visibly engulfed her.

He'd never been so proud of anyone in his entire

life; he was nearly bursting with the force of it. "*That's the girl I wanted to see. You're a fighter, Elle; never forget it. Malcolm can't take from you what you refuse to let him have.*"

She stood stock still, her gaze assessing as she worked to calm her breathing. At that moment, the sun crested over the horizon, illuminating the pride in her eyes. God, but she was gorgeous. Had anyone ever looked more beautiful with messy hair and a dirt-streaked face?

"If you tell me," she said sternly, "that this was all meant to teach me some sort of lesson, I may very well plunge this foil into your heart, Nicolas Norton."

He chuckled before dragging his sleeve over his sweaty forehead. "Bloodthirsty wench." Grabbing her foible, he pulled the weapon from her grasp. She didn't fight him, easily surrendering her hold. He dropped it to the ground beside his own, and held out his hand to her. "Come here."

"I will not," she said, straightening her shoulders imperiously. "In case you didn't notice, I won."

It was all he could do not to tug her into his arms right then. "Yes, and as such, you may collect your spoils, same as I always have." He turned his cheek, screwing up his face just as she invariably did whenever he claimed his prize, pretending he didn't want her to kiss him.

Hoping like hell she would.

Her laughter was full of delight, heady in its sweetness. "Do you know, Mr. Norton, for the first time in you life, I think you may have earned a kiss."

***

Eleanor stepped toward him, feeling strong and in control in a way she hadn't in days. Years perhaps. Nothing was solved, but hope had been renewed. Faith in herself had been restored. She could at least try for another solution. Nick had given her that much, and for that she adored him.

For the next few moments, at least—then they could return to being adversaries.

With his damp shirt plastered to his body, he looked every bit the gladiator, standing tall and proud on the heels of victory. Ironic, considering he had lost, but still somehow fitting. She hadn't been exaggerating—he had truly earned a reward.

As she leaned forward, his chest rose with a sharp

intake of air. She flicked her gaze from his cheek to his expression, and froze, only inches away. His green eyes were burning, his lips slightly parted. Awareness washed over her, cascading through her veins and landing deep in her belly. All at once the moment took on a whole new meaning.

She wasn't just sharing an innocent moment with her step-cousin. She was standing almost chest-to-chest with a tall, powerful, handsome-as-sin man.

Alone.

Her heart slammed against her ribs, pounding harder than it had during their entire match. His smell was familiar, his eyes exactly as they had always been, but somehow everything seemed different.

Slowly, deliberately he turned his head until they faced each other directly, the very air they breathed mingling in the narrow space between them. The morning light caressed them as they stood completely still, unable to look away. She knew it should feel wrong—this was Nicolas!—but nothing had ever felt more natural.

Her eyes dropped to his lips. For once they were without any hint of that rakish smile with which he so loved to torture her. He'd always seemed so young, but all she could see right then was the man he had become.

A man her very heart seemed to be beating for.

And yet, still neither of them moved. A sixth sense told her that as soon as they did, nothing would ever be the same. He would never again be little Nick, thorn in her side. Uncertainty warred with unfamiliar passion, and she dragged her gaze up to meet his, helpless as to what to do.

For a moment, she thought he would act, pressing his lips to hers and releasing the desire that both tantalized and terrified her. She held her breath, afraid to so much as blink. How was it possible she could want something so badly, and at the same time want to escape, to run from the emotions she wasn't prepared for?

Finally, he closed his eyes and exhaled, surely every drop of air from his lungs. When he opened them again, it was as if a curtain had been drawn shut. "Fine, fine—I'll give you a reprieve. I know deep down you're just afraid you'll never measure up to my outstanding kisses." His voice was hoarse, but the smile was firmly in place. "Now off with you, before someone discovers us and ruins all our fun."

He was right. Already, the sun was well above the horizon, the sky transitioning from reds to pinks.

Nodding, she bent to retrieve her foil, trying to convince herself that it was relief, not regret, that wilted her shoulders. Whatever madness had seized her, it was gone now.

Or so she told herself.

Turning on her heel, she hurried toward the dirt path that led to the house, wanting to put distance between them, to cut the odd connection that even now tempted her to turn back.

With her future at stake, she simply couldn't afford to be diverted by the man who had long been her opponent, but who now seemed like so much more.

Chapter Six

God in heaven, *what* had just happened?

Nick slumped down the wall, dropping to his backside and letting his head fall back against the cool stones of the old tumbledown wall. His blood still roared in his ears—as well as in other places—and he raked his hands through his hair, digging his fingers into his scalp.

What the hell was wrong with him? If she had any clue how he truly felt about her, she'd never allow them to be alone together again. Perhaps not even in the same bloody room. He gave a humorless laugh. How could he have let his control slip so thoroughly?

Because of her.

For the first time in fifteen years, she had been about to kiss him. Of her own prerogative. When she'd declared her intention, he'd been so surprised, he couldn't stop his reaction. How could he? It was something he'd dreamed about for so long, he couldn't bloody well remember a time he *hadn't* wanted it.

But this wasn't about him. It wasn't about the desire coursing through his body, or the secret longing he had hid so effectively for years. This was about Eleanor having what *she* wanted in life; or more to the point, what she didn't want: a husband.

He closed his eyes, shaking his head back and forth. He'd do whatever it took to protect her from getting hurt. Yes, he wanted to instill self-confidence in her once more, but after that near kiss, he wasn't leaving anything to chance. He'd be damned if he'd let another man claim her against her will.

If Malcolm thought he could strong arm her into doing his bidding, he had another thing coming. The trick was Nick had to come up with a way to keep her from being married off, without giving Malcolm the chance to blame her.

Drawing in a deep breath, he came to his feet and straightened his shoulders. It was time to go to battle.

***

If Uncle Robert sent one more self-satisfied look in

her and Lord Henry's direction, Eleanor was going to scream, right there in the middle of Miss Landon's song. And wouldn't *that* put a damper on his plans. She allowed a small smile at the thought.

The earl leaned closer from his seat to the right of her and murmured uncomfortably close to her ear, "I'm so pleased to see you enjoying yourself, Miss Abbington. My late wife, bless her, never was one for these sorts of amusements." He fluttered a hand in the vicinity of his forehead. "Megrims."

Possibly. Eleanor was more inclined to believe the dearly departed countess was simply more skilled at escaping his company than she. She nodded politely and leaned away as inconspicuously as she could manage.

It wasn't that he was unkind, but he possessed the conversation skills of a parrot. Not to mention he seemed to think her eyes were located somewhere in the region of her breasts, or the fact that he was exceptionally fond of onions, the evidence of which emanated from him like a fog.

She really didn't dislike him, but the idea of marriage to him made her physically ill. And blast it all, Nicolas was right. She didn't have to bow to Uncle Robert's demands, nor did her sister have to suffer the consequences. There had to be a way to get around them, and she wouldn't rest until she figured out what that was. Perhaps she should have shared with Nick exactly what she was dealing with. He'd surprised her a lot since returning home; maybe he'd be able to surprise her again by coming up with a solution.

For perhaps the tenth time since the recital began, Eleanor cut her gaze toward the side wall, where he stood alone, watching the performance. She still had no idea what to make of what had happened between them this morning. Or more accurately, what *hadn't* happened. All she knew for certain was that every time she thought of him, her cheeks heated and a shower of sparks seemed to cascade through her middle.

As if he sensed her thoughts, Nick shifted his gaze, catching her with God knew what expression on her face. She jerked her attention back to the front of the room, her heart beating like mad. Good heavens, she had to get hold of herself. She was acting like a proper fool there in the drawing room for anyone to see.

And truly, there were much more important things to think about.

Beside her, Aunt Margaret hummed along with the music, her head bobbing in time with the pianoforte tune. Eleanor still didn't know what to do about her aunt. It was a sort of betrayal, knowing that her own mother's sister had thought her hopeless these past few years. They were supposed to be each other's support.

The song came to an end, and Miss Landon curtseyed prettily as the guests clapped. Eleanor stood, hoping to steal a few moments for herself, but Lord Henry blocked her way. "Miss Abbington," he said, his cheeks oddly ruddy, "Would you care to step out onto the terrace with me? The night air shall do us both good after an evening indoors."

Drat it all—why couldn't he see she wasn't interested in spending time with him? Not that she could overtly offend him, but still, one would think her disinterest would speak for itself. "Oh, how kind. But my aunt and I were just about to take a turn about the room." She widened her eyes at her aunt, willing her to go along. It had just come out—a holdover from when she could rely on Aunt Margaret's support.

Blinking in surprise, the older woman hesitated for an instant before turning a bright smile to Lord Henry. "Yes, yes, I thought a bit of exercise would be just the thing after sitting for so long."

Eleanor sighed. Thank goodness.

"There you are, dear sister," Uncle Robert cut in, sidling up behind them. "I wonder if I might steal you away for a moment. I have . . . something that I wish to discuss." Though he smiled cordially, his eyes were sharp enough to cut glass. "Lord Henry, you wouldn't mind keeping my niece company, would you?"

"Delighted, old man. I was just saying a bit of air on the terrace sounded like just the thing." He lifted a brow at Eleanor. "Shall we?"

Blast, blast, blast. To refuse would be the height of rudeness. Now was not the time to make a scene. Dipping her head in reluctant agreement, she said, "Indeed."

As she and Lord Henry started for the doors, her eyes met with Nick's. He stood beside Miss Landon as she chattered away, her cheeks rosy and her face alight with delight. Eleanor felt the heat of his gaze all the way to her toes, but then he abruptly turned away, severing the connection as he gave his whole attention to his companion.

Hurt flooded her heart even as she smiled her thanks to Lord Henry for opening the door for her. Despite herself, she'd been begging Nick to help, to somehow intervene. She had no right to be upset, but it still stung that he had turned his back on her—literally.

Warm, sweetly fragranced air greeted her as she stepped outside. She allowed Lord Henry to guide her to the ornamental balustrade overlooking the rose garden, which, thanks to a series of torches along the outer wall, was well enough lit so as to not seem overly intimate.

"Miss Abbington," he said, surprising her by boldly taking her gloved hand in his. "It's no secret I came to this party with an eye toward beginning the search for my next wife. With only my three daughters, I am still very much in need of an heir. At my age, the thought of marrying a young debutant seems a somewhat distasteful. You, on the other hand, have the maturity and lineage to be quite an appropriate match."

Even through her growing alarm, Eleanor still managed to be insulted. Yes, at four-and-twenty she was the perfect match for a man with four and a half decades under his belt. Gently but firmly she tried to extract her hand from his grasp, to no avail.

Chuckling indulgently, he said, "No need to worry, my dear. I have already spoken with your uncle, and obtained his permission to ask you to be my wife. Such an intimacy is to be expected." He lowered his head slightly, and she exhaled in an effort to ward off the smell of his breath. "Besides, Malcolm told me how favorably inclined you were to accept my suit. I'm honored that you think well enough of me to approach your uncle about such a thing."

Alarm catapulted into panic as her blood turned to ice. She was supposed to have more time—she wasn't properly prepared yet.

"Lord Henry, I . . . " Her mind went blank as she desperately cast about for a proper response—one that would *not* result in a betrothal announcement.

He squeezed her hand and grinned. "I can see you are quite beside yourself. To be expected, I think. Perhaps we shall bypass words for a moment."

Bypass words? What did— Oh heaven help her, he was leaning in for a kiss. Eleanor tensed, her mind flailing about for a way to escape.

"There you are."

The sharp, jovial words made them startle apart, and Eleanor stumbled backward a few steps, desperate for space. Nick stood at the door, outlined by the blazing candles of the drawing room behind him. He stepped toward them, his muscled shoulders ramrod straight and his hands clasped behind his back. His features were arranged in polite greeting, but his eyes blazed in the torchlight. "Lord Henry, my stepfather asked that I retrieve you. He had a most pressing matter which he feels must be discussed at once."

Eleanor sucked in great gusts of air, trying to regain her composure. Nick had never looked more handsome, more like a savior than he did in that moment, especially with his smart crimson army dress jacket.

"Now? Can you tell him I'll be in momentarily?" Henry sounded as befuddled as she felt.

Nick lifted his chin in a gesture designed to showcase his authority. "I'm afraid he was most insistent, my lord. I'll wait here with my cousin while you see to him. She'll be here when you return."

For the first time, Eleanor could imagine him dressing down one of his men. He emanated power and superiority with little more than a stern expression and commanding voice. Henry glanced back at Eleanor for a moment, clearly unsure of what to do. She found a smile, heaven knew where from, and nodded encouragingly. "Do hurry back."

She held her breath as he hesitated, willing him to leave. A moment later he relented. "Very well. I'll be only a moment." He offered a dip of his head before hurrying inside.

Oh thank God. She released her breath, sagging against the balustrade. That had been a very near thing. She turned her attention to her unlikely hero and offered him a wan smile. "I shall never be able to repay you for your timing. Or Uncle Robert's timing, I suppose."

He stepped closer to her, tilting his head but never taking his eyes from her. "Oh? And why is that?"

"Because he just asked me to *marry* him," she exclaimed, putting a hand to her heart. "I, I didn't know what to say, and then he was leaning toward me and I was so flustered that I didn't know what to do and then . . ." She trailed off, shaking her head.

He took another step. "And then . . .?"

She sucked in a cleansing breath and peered up at him. "You were there."

His eyes were piercing in the near darkness. "Because you needed me."

"Yes. But I thought . . ." She pictured him, turning away from her pleas as she'd silently begged for his help.

"What did you think?"

Her heart pounded and she couldn't even say why. "That you turned your back on me. That you put me from your mind." But she'd been wrong. He was here now, there when she needed him most.

"Never," he said, the single word rife with conviction. "But I did have to make my excuses." He stepped nearer still, bringing them at once entirely too close together and not nearly close enough. He lifted her hand from the stone railing and guided her around so she stood between him and the house.

The torchlight danced in his eyes and bathed his skin in a warm, golden glow. He looked . . . determined. Decided. But not altogether sure of himself. Instead of releasing her hand, he raised it to his lips and placed a soft, gentle kiss to her knuckles. Awareness raced down her back in a flurry of gooseflesh—he had never done such a thing before. His kisses were to mock, not to soothe. To tease and provoke, never to show care or affection.

The old Nick, the one who had left two years ago and gone to the army, was fading fast from her memory. In his place was this man. Capable of tenderness and seriousness. Of being her champion.

When he lifted his head, his gaze flicked to just over her shoulder before meeting hers. "Do you trust me?"

There was an edge to his voice that wasn't there

moments earlier. "Should I?" She didn't know what he was asking, but she knew instinctually that it was important.

"Probably not."

A ghost of a smile slipped over her lips. "Then you should not ask it of me."

"Then can you at least forgive me?" he asked, lacing his fingers with hers with an urgency that made her pulse quicken.

Forgive him? Confusion at his words warred with an unexpected rush of desire at his touch, robbing her of her wits. "What—"

But he didn't give her a chance to complete her sentence. With a sharp tug, he pulled her flat against his chest and before she could do little more than gasp, his lips crashed down upon hers. A thousand butterflies set flight in her stomach—her first kiss! She moaned with the pure pleasure of it. His lips were deliciously warm, and fit against hers as if they'd been molded for each other. The smell of his skin was like a drug, sending ribbons of pleasure through her whole body.

It was perfection. Even better, if that was possible.

Her Nicolas, her opponent for so many years had somehow turned into the man who made her heart sing and her toes curl with one utterly searing kiss.

He guided her hands to the hard plane of his upper chest, pressing them in place before dropping his own hold to her waist. He pulled back slightly and whispered against her lips, "I'm sorry."

Sorry? Bewilderment stilled her body, and a heartbeat later he launched himself backwards, as if pushed by an unseen force. She blinked, her eyes wide as she struggled to make sense out of what was happening.

"Good God," a male voice roared from behind her, "What is the meaning of this?"

Chapter Seven

*I*f looks could kill, Nick would have been a smoldering pile of ashes on the flagstone. Malcolm nearly glowed with red hot anger, his face contorted with the force of his fury. Beside him Lord Henry stood frozen, his shock congealing into horror. Already faces were appearing in the window as people rushed to see what the disturbance was about.

Nick picked himself up off the ground and brushed off his soiled clothes. "Malcolm, Henry."

"Explain yourself," his stepfather demanded, stalking over to where Eleanor leaned against the railing, both hands covering her mouth.

Nick couldn't meet her eyes. Not yet. Shrugging, he said, "I thought to steal a kiss. The lady thought otherwise." His tone was lazy, insolent even, despite the emotion burning in his veins.

The kiss was meant to be a means to an end: ruin Eleanor's marriage prospect, *without* her taking any blame. To let Malcolm's wrath fall on *his* head, not hers. But that was before their lips touched. Before the whole world had so completely ceased to exist, and the woman he had loved for years had actually leaned into the kiss. Before he'd tasted her, or felt her thundering heartbeat.

"I ought to—"

"*Lord Malcolm*," Aunt Margaret interrupted, pushing through the crowd to where they stood. "Perhaps this is a discussion to be held in private."

She put her arm around Eleanor and tried to guide her away, but Ellie resisted. "No, I should go with them. This isn't what it looks like."

Nick started to speak, to say something that would keep her from ruining his efforts, but Aunt Margaret beat him to it. "Not now, dear," the older woman said through gritted teeth. "You'll have time for that later." She forcefully pushed Eleanor to the house, glancing back only once before disappearing inside. He'd never seen Eleanor's skin so pale, and for a moment guilt assailed him.

No, he refused to feel guilty. He knew when he came out here that he would be hurting the rest of his family, as well as Eleanor. But he could think of no other plan to free her from Malcolm's dictates. There would be hell to pay—his stepfather would make sure of it—but Nick would not regret this night.

"In my study," Malcolm ground out, then turned on his heel and marched inside.

Obedient as a lapdog, Nick followed behind him, allowing a small self-satisfied grin to curl his lips as he walked through the gathered guests. He had a part to play: ruinous rake, not to be trusted with delicate English maidens.

They passed his mother as they strode through the drawing room. Her eyes were red, her gaze unfocused as she smiled in confusion at the pair of them. She raised her glass, saying after them, "My two favorite men, together at last," before draining the contents in one drink.

Drunk again—what a bloody surprise. She never had been there to stand up for him when he was growing up, when the disdain for her own husband had nearly crushed him. Why should anything change now?

Once in the study, the door hadn't even clicked closed before Malcolm turned on him, eyes burning with fiery resentment. "You filthy bastard—you did this on purpose."

"Purposely kissed her? Yes, no denying that."

Malcolm slammed a palm against the surface of his desk. "Ruined her chances with Henry! You could have kissed her a thousand times in a thousand different places—you purposely set out to destroy what I worked so hard to bring together."

"'What God hath brought together, let no man set asunder?' Sorry, but your plans had little consequence on my actions, old man."

"This is all some sort of bloody game to you, isn't it? See what you can do to drag the Earl of Malcolm down to your level?"

Of course he would think that. As if Nick had ever wanted anything for or from the man, other than a little respect. Perhaps a kind word or two. Instead, all he'd had was ill-concealed disgust. "Oh, looks like you caught me."

"You pathetic excuse for a man. Congratulations, you've made me a laughingstock. Any hope of Eleanor making a good match has been destroyed."

Good. "Come now—I wouldn't say that. Now that I have claimed the fair maiden's kiss, I suppose *I* could marry her." His chest tightened as if wrapped with steel bands. He'd love nothing more than to do exactly that, just as he knew Eleanor would like nothing less. By making such a statement, there was no better way to insure that Malcolm would *never* let it happen.

Nostrils flaring like a taunted bull, Malcolm shook his head in disgust. "Over my dead body. You've always been jealous of the natural children of this family. You never could handle the fact they are superior to you in every way possible."

Nick bit down on his tongue, hard. William, Libby, and Eleanor were the best things that had ever happened to him. Despite the fact William was years younger and given all the privilege his status as heir required, he had never been anything but a brother to Nick. As for Eleanor . . . This was all for her. He had to hold his tongue, no matter how much he ached to fight back.

Nick tilted his head as if considering the charge, then shrugged. "Perhaps."

Malcolm stilled. "I should call you out. If it wasn't political suicide, I would do just that."

Doubtful; Malcolm knew he could never win in a duel with Nick.

The earl walked behind his desk and sat, inspecting Nick as if he were the foulest of creatures. "As of this moment, you are expelled from this family. I hereby banish you from this house and from any other property I own. If you try to step foot on even a square inch of my land, I will have you thrown in gaol. Furthermore, I forbid you to see your mother, or any other member of this family."

A boulder settled deep in Nick's gut, making it hard to breath. He gritted his teeth, struggling to maintain a neutral expression. If this was the price of restoring Eleanor's choices for her own life, than so be it.

Malcolm leaned forward over his desk, resting his elbows on the polished wood and lacing his fingers in front of him. "And lastly," he said, a hint of malevolent pleasure lifting one side of his lip in a sneer, "a letter will go out in tomorrow's post addressed to my solicitor. By this time next week, your commission will have been sold.

"Welcome to the life you *should* have had, Norton. I hope you choke on it."

***

Aunt Margaret paced from one side of the room to the other, her face drawn with worry as her fingers mangled a lace handkerchief. "I don't understand,

Eleanor. Why on earth would he have done such a thing? Ruining your chances like that," she said, shaking her head. "He has always been a bit of a scoundrel, but I always felt he was a gentleman at heart."

Heedless of her fine silk gown, Eleanor sat in a heap on the settee, pressing a pillow to her middle. The myriad of emotions rushing through her all at once made it hard to think, let alone make sense of what had just happened. What should she do? What did this mean for her sister and her?

Her heart ached bitterly. What on earth had Nicholas been thinking? She wouldn't be surprised if Malcolm met him at dawn over this. Peering up to her aunt, she shook her head. "He was trying to save me."

If only she had told Nicolas the whole truth of the situation. Eleanor squeezed her eyes shut. He may have had some ridiculous notion of helping her, but what if Libby was the one forced to pay the price?

Aunt Margaret stopped dead in her tracks. "*Save* you? From what?"

"From having to marry Lord Henry."

She blinked, dumbfounded. "But you *wanted* to marry. You told me yourself you were finally interested."

105

It was Eleanor's turn to be at a loss. "What? No, I didn't want to marry. Uncle Robert was forcing me to. You know how I feel about marriage after Mama and Papa."

Aunt Margaret put a hand to her mouth. She looked beyond appalled. "Oh my dear! I had no idea. I thought at long last you had changed your mind. I thought you had finally seen the goodness marriage can hold."

She'd been on Eleanor's side after all? Something inside of her eased, making things just a little less awful. "No—I mean, I'm sure that it can be, but I never wanted to risk it."

"Then why—?"

"Because Uncle threatened that if I didn't, he would summon Libby from school, forcing her to marry instead." The words burned her throat like whisky.

The fury in her aunt's eyes was a balm to her soul. "Over my dead body."

Eleanor gasped—it was the most passion she'd seen in her aunt since Mama died. She seemed fully alive again, like the formidable woman she had once been.

"He ruined your mother's life by forcing her to marry your father. She was determined that you and your sister would not suffer the same fate. Before your debut, she made Robert swear that you and Libby would be free to choose your own husbands—if you even wanted one at all."

Eleanor swallowed against the emotion that clogged her throat. Mama had done that for her?

A small, unexpected smile deepened the lines bracketing her aunt's thin lips. "She threatened if he didn't, she would marry a Whig and take up the plight of the working class, handing out pamphlets on the street if need be. She would have done it too, I swear to it. Robert realized it as well; I was right there when he finally gave his word."

He had agreed? He had given Eleanor's mother his word, only to break it the moment it suited him? Anger flared to life deep within her, heating her blood and searing her resolve. She thought of Nick, standing up for her in his own convoluted way, now being subjected to her uncle's fury.

This wasn't his fight—it was hers. It was past time Uncle Robert was subjected to *her* wrath, not the other way around. Hadn't Nick just shown her how strong she could be? "I have to go," she said suddenly, unable to sit idle for even one more moment.

"Wait."

She stopped at the authoritative tone in the older woman's voice. "Yes?"

Tilting her head, Aunt Margaret leveled a thoughtful gaze on Eleanor. "I understand now why rescue was necessary in the case of Lord Henry. But I still don't know why Nick decided he was the one to do it. Are not the two of you adversaries?"

And there was the crux of the matter.

An unfamiliar longing wrapped around her heart as she thought of him and what exactly he was to her. What they were to each other. "Oh Aunt, I've been so stupid. All this time we bickered and argued, but yet all along . . ." she shook her head helplessly. "It's been him. It's always been him. The one who drives me mad, who makes me want to throttle him, but who always challenged me. Always looked to me as an equal." She swallowed as a new truth assailed her with the force of an exploding firework. "I can't bear the thought of being without him."

"So you didn't mind his kiss?"

Heat scorched her cheeks, but she looked her aunt straight in the eye. "I loved it. And I love him."

Aunt Margaret's mouth dropped open in surprise, even as her eyes misted over. Nodding crisply, she rose to her feet. "I'm coming with you. And next time," she said, tossing a shawl about her shoulders before linking arms with Eleanor, "do feel free to come to me when my brother makes an arse of himself."

***

Nick stood rigidly still, absorbing the ramifications of his own stepfather's words. His commission. His livelihood—his very identity. These were to be the price for Eleanor's freedom.

So be it.

Though dread filled him like rising flood waters, there was no regret. No remorse at all. She was worth any price, as far as he was concerned. He forced his lips into a grin as he addressed his hateful step-father. "Ah, the relief you must feel to finally wash your hands of me. See now? I did you a favor after all."

"Too bad such a thing didn't happen a decade ago," the earl retorted. "You have ten minutes to be gone from this house before I have you thrown out."

Nick nodded once in acknowledgement, then turned and strode for the door. As he reached for the knob, the door swung open, and Eleanor nearly bowled him over. He jumped back, regaining his balance even as he lost his breath. His heart soared at the sight of her. Her face was a mask of determination, her head held high and her eyes flashing like fire-lit bronze.

His beautiful, glorious warrior—God how he loved her.

Malcolm started to protest, but she sliced a hand through the air, silencing him. She marched straight past Nick to the desk, Aunt Margaret following behind her. "How dare you, sir. You made a promise to my mother, and she's not even gone a year before you break it? What kind of man are you?"

Malcolm's face contorted, going as red as the scarlet curtains behind him. "How dare I? How dare *you*, bursting in here like some sort of lowborn, mannerless chit. Margaret, escort our niece to her room. I will deal with you both later."

Instead of jumping to his bidding, Aunt Margaret crossed her arms in a show of protest. "I do believe I'd like to hear what the girl has to say, dear brother. Eleanor?"

Well done, Aunt Margaret! Nick stared in shock at his normally impeccably-mannered aunt. And he wasn't the only one. From behind his desk, Malcolm sputtered in outrage, unable to even come up with a proper response.

"Thank you, Aunt," Eleanor said primly before returning her full attention to her uncle. Her spine was ramrod straight, her chin lifted and her shoulders back. "Listen to me, and listen well. If you think today's scene reflected badly upon you, you can't even imagine what I will do if you so much as harm one hair on Nicolas's head, or seek to injure his prospects."

She took a step closer to the desk, forcing Malcolm to look up to her. "I will happily bring shame to this entire family if it means making you pay for what you did to my mother, and what you tried to do to me and my sister."

Her gaze jerked to Nick. "What has he promised as punishment? Are you to duel?"

"Er, no," he replied, momentarily caught off guard. Absurdly, he had to bite back the grin that threatened to emerge. She was just so damn magnificent. Straightening his face, he said, "Merely permanent alienation from this family, and the revocation of the funds for my commission. Nothing I can't handle," he added, not wanting her to think it was too great a penalty for him to bear.

"No, nothing you *will* handle," she said, her eyes

fairly glowing with passion. She'd never been so self-assured; it was all he could not to applaud her. Her hands to her hips, she turned back to Malcolm. "Nick attempted to rescue me from the fate you tried to manufacture, but this is my fight, not his.

"So here are your choices, dear uncle. Either I go back to the party and make a scene you will not soon forget, or you go in there and announce that, much to your surprise, your niece and step-son have made a love match, and will be married in one month's time. Oh, and my entire dowry will be transferred upon our marriage."

It took a moment for Nick to realize that the echoing gasp was his. "No, Eleanor, I won't allow you to be trapped—"

She whirled to face him, her eyes flashing and her color high. "You mean married to you?"

Married to Eleanor. He clenched his teeth together, ruthlessly squelching the surge of hope her words evoked. Everything he had done tonight was to protect her from exactly that fate. "Yes," he answered, unable to keep the desperation from his voice.

She shook her head, looking up to him with soulful brown eyes. "What choice do I have? You have ruined me."

Chapter Eight

*E*leanor waited for the shock of the statement to sink in before stepping forward and taking Nick's hands in her own. "Yes, you ruined me in the eyes of the *ton*, but that's not what I mean. Nick, you have ruined me for any other man. You've ruined me for living the life I once enjoyed."

She met his gaze directly, wanting him to see the truth in her eyes, to know that she meant what she said. "You have shown true valor, you have treated me with respect, and you've shown that my wishes are as close to your heart as your own.

"I never thought I could bear to be married, but now I know that I can't bear *not* to be. I can't fathom being without you. And I must know," she said, her voice raw with the emotion that consumed her, "after that kiss, have I ruined you as well?"

He looked down at her, his green eyes giving away nothing. "No," he said, shaking his head decisively.

"*No?*" Her heart squeezed painfully in her chest, taking the breath from her lungs. Had she lost her gamble? Had she been wrong about the kiss, and the connection she felt between them?

"You ruined me with the *first* kiss," he said, squeezing her fingers tightly in his. "Eleanor Josephine Abbington, I have loved you since the day we met. One look at those huge brown eyes and the challenge you presented, and I was lost."

He couldn't be serious! He'd loved her all these years? She shook her head, unable to believe what he was saying. "But all the teasing, and insults, and pestering . . ."

For the first time that evening, a smile came to his lips. "When a fatherless, friendless boy is set before the gorgeous older granddaughter of an earl, what hope does he have? None – other than to keep the girl well enough engaged that she can't possibly ignore him, even if she wanted to."

She simply stared at him, unable to process the emotions welling up inside her like a cyclone. Happiness, incredulousness, joy, love, disbelief—it was impossible to untangle one from the other.

The moment was broken when Uncle Robert came suddenly to his feet, knocking his chair back with a clatter. "Enough! If you think I am going to bow to your whims like some sort of coward—"

"*Not* a coward," Aunt Margaret broke in. "A wise man. One who knows when he's been beat. One who will salvage the evening exactly as presented, so that his precious bill, and the support of those influential men out there, will not be compromised."

"I will no—"

"You *will*." The steel in her voice was unmistakable. "I may not have been here to help my sister, but by God I will help her daughters. And let me just say, the scene Eleanor promises will be nothing compared to the scandal you would see from me if you ever threaten any of my nieces or nephews again."

Eleanor's heart nearly burst for the woman beside her. She slipped her hand into her aunt's and squeezed.

The fury on her uncle's face would have scared her before, but not anymore. He had no sway over her, and he never again would. And, judging by the way his jaw worked as he ground his teeth, he knew it, too. Finally, he said, "I will make the announcement. I will sign over the dowry. But I will never, ever have the two of you step foot on my property again. In fact, I wish never to see your faces again."

Victory! Squeezing both her aunt's and her betrothed's hands hard, Eleanor nodded. "Agreed."

Marching straight past them, Malcolm stormed from the room without another word.

Releasing her death grip on the others' hands, the three of them joined in a spontaneous hug.

"Have no fear," Aunt Margaret said. "I hereby exempt my home from his restrictions. Now, I believe I'll go find your mother, Nicolas."

Alone at last.

Suddenly shy, Eleanor bit her lip and pivoted to face the man who had turned her whole life upside down in a matter of days.

Smiling, he slipped his hands to her waist. "Now, my prickly sweet Ellie, I have a question for you. Will," he kissed her forehead, "you," then her nose, "marry," he lingered over her lips, "me?"

Laughter bubbled up within her, completely eradicating all the negative emotions that had brewed inside her for days. "I thought we already agreed."

His brows snapped together in mock affront. "I will

not accept a proposal issued from you through my stepfather. Now, answer the question."

Her joy was so complete as to be all consuming. "If you are mad enough to marry me, my love, then I am likewise inclined."

He flashed a huge, genuine grin, all arrogance and mocking forever gone. He wrapped his arms fully around her waist and lifted her from her feet, spinning them both in a quick, dizzying circle before pressing his lips firmly upon hers, despite their laughter.

She encircled his neck with her arms, holding him as closely to her as she possibly could. Her sweet, infuriating, irresistible Nicolas. When the kiss ended, she pulled back slightly and smiled down into his eyes. "You do realize that Uncle Robert is serious about disowning us."

"Thank God," he replied, his green eyes sparkling. "My plan may have taken a decade or two, but it finally paid off."

"Oh, so I'm a means to an end, am I?" she teased.

"Indeed . . . the means to a *happy* ending."

Epilogue

"*J* ust what do you think you are doing?"

Eleanor froze mid-lunge, her foil extended straight out in front of her. Blast, she was caught. The babbling brook that had so enchanted her when they purchased their small estate had apparently masked the sounds of her husband's approach. Biting her lip, she straightened and turned to face the music. Nick stood behind her, partially shrouded in the heavy sheet of early morning fog, his arms crossed and his brow raised expectantly.

She offered a bright smile, all innocence. "Morning constitutional?"

He let his hands fall to his hips, giving her a very nice view of his chest through the partially-buttoned, generously-cut white shirt. "Uh huh." He started forward, closing the distance between them with four easy strides. "You, madam, know full well you are not to be out here like this."

Even as he pinned her with his sternest expression, his lips still curled with a hint of that delicious smile of his. Her heart gave a little flip. Almost a year of marriage, and he still could take her breath away.

He stopped an arm's length away and held out his hand. "Your weapon?"

Scrunching her nose, she tucked the foil into the crook of her elbow. "Don't be silly, Nicolas. There's nothing wrong with a little exercise. In fact, I think it's good."

He flapped his hand open and closed in the universal sign for *hand it over*. "The doctor said no strenuous activities."

"Oh really," she said, lifting an imperious brow. "If I recall correctly, you were quite enthusiastic about our *strenuous activities* last night."

Nick gave a bark of laughter and shook his head. "Oh, sure—use *that* against me." Chuckling, he slipped a hand over her shoulder and tugged her in for a kiss, foil and all. She sighed happily, readily leaning into his embrace.

When he pulled back, he placed a tender hand to

her middle. The warmth of his bare fingers seeping through the fabric of her fencing shirt was nothing compared to the warmth of his gaze. "I know it's very early yet, but put a poor soldier's mind at ease, and do please stick to *walking* for your constitutionals."

She loved when he looked at her like that, as though she were the most precious treasure in the world. Because of that look, she had taken the biggest risk of her life—throwing years of caution to the wind in order to be with him—and it had paid off beyond her wildest dreams. A husband who loved, respected, and cherished her, a much longed for baby on the way, and all the family members who really mattered—Aunt Margaret, Libby, and William—by their sides, refusing to be intimidated by Uncle Robert's wrath.

She was happier than she'd ever been in her life, and she had one person to thank for it.

Covering his hand with her own, she sighed and nodded. "Fine, fine. Have it your way. But I warn you— I shall hold you accountable for keeping me entertained for the next seven or so months."

His smile was slow and devilish and full of promise. "Deal."

In one smooth move, he divested her of the foil

and lifted her into his arms, making her laugh out loud. "Nicholas!" she gasped, clinging to his neck as he started back for the house.

"What?" he said mildly, not the least bit winded as he navigated the rocky uphill path. "I take my promises very seriously. If it is entertainment you want, it is entertainment you shall have."

Grinning, Eleanor settled into his arms, relishing the familiar smell of his skin and the feel of his muscled arms around her. There was no other place on earth she'd rather be. "Thank you," she whispered, the simple words filled with a wealth of emotion.

He slowed and tilted his head so he could meet her gaze. "Whatever for?"

"For making me the happiest person in all of England."

His arms tightened around her as he brushed a soft kiss against her lips. "My dear Ellie," he said, his voice slightly gruff. "I'm merely returning the favor."

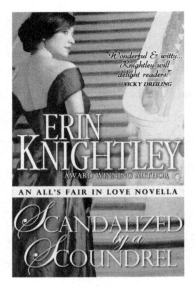

Don't miss

Scandalized by a Scoundrel

the next novella in the

All's Fair in Love Series!

About the Author

Despite being an avid reader and closet writer her whole life, Erin Knightley decided to pursue a sensible career in science. It was only after earning her B.S. and working in the field for years that she realized doing the sensible thing wasn't any fun at all. Following her dreams, Erin left her practical side behind and now spends her days writing. Together with her tall, dark, and handsome husband and their three spoiled mutts, she is living her own Happily Ever After in North Carolina.

Find her at www.ErinKnightley.com, on Twitter.com/ErinKnightley, or at facebook.com/ErinKnightley

Made in the USA
Coppell, TX
30 June 2020

29797643R00075